DEATH

RE-ENACTED

The Possumwood Mysteries Book 4

HOLLY DEY

Acknowledgements

I couldn't do this without the love and support of my wonderful family. I love you so much!

Chapter 1

"Alright, get out your pyrrole red—we're going to paint some blood. Maybe. Who knows—you might need some blue."

"I only have Winsor red," retired homicide detective Primrose Corvina Donovan, who preferred to go by PC, muttered under her breath. Windsor would have to do. It was an hour's drive from Possumwood all the way back to Houston, to an art supply shop.

Wilma Gatewood, the acrylics instructor, uncovered a large, framed picture propped on an easel at the front of the classroom at the back of *The Best Little Art Gallery in Texas*. "This is a print of the *Battle of Mirabella Creek*, done by an actual participant, our own renowned Francois de Lamartine. Now, the citizens of Possumwood stayed put during the Runaway Scrape, and missed most of the terrors in the war for Texas Independence, except this one little skirmish."

Lamartine. Wasn't he the French diplomat that built the mayor's house? PC studied the painting. A dozen or so ragged Mexican cavalry rode on the left side of the creek, and perhaps five times as many Texians marched on the right, armed with pitchforks, flintlocks, and axes. The soldiers, too, had rifles, but perhaps they had spent all their ammunition at the Alamo, as the guns remained in their saddle holsters. The officer leading the charge brandished his saber as his furious bay horse reared. Even the water in the stream seemed angry, as it boiled and foamed, slopping out of its steep banks. A lone blue jay, a bright pop of cobalt amidst the other muted colors, surveyed the conflict from the safety of a possumwood tree full of cream-colored persimmon flowers.

It looked like a typical nineteenth century battle painting—dour, windblown people on angry horses underneath distant, misty clouds—except for one thing. In the bottom left corner, a woman in a pale blue dress placidly emptied an ash bucket into a tub, seemingly oblivious to the imminent battle in front of her.

Wilma adjusted the easel. "Now, I'd like you to think about what happens next. Do the soldiers retreat? Is there a battle? Does the bird take flight? Use color and contrast to add meaning—and I'm not expecting you to try to create the entire next scene from a full 36" x 48" painting! Of course not—we only have an hour and a half. Just hone in on a section that speaks to you and paint that detail."

The woman in the painting really struck PC. *Was that really the best time to empty her bucket of ashes?* So, that's what the detective painted. Except in her version, she stood upright, an empty pail dangling from one hand. PC wasn't particularly good with faces, so she chose a more impressionist style. She was just finishing up the portrait by adding a little blood spatter to the oblivious woman's clothes when Wilma paused at her seat.

"It's interesting you chose her. Why?"

PC shrugged. "She seemed out of place."

"Yes. That is one of the idiosyncrasies of de Lamartine. In every painting, he has this lady in blue doing something that just doesn't belong with the rest of the picture. Some people say she and her quirks are clues."

PC put her brushes into the cup of water in front of her. "I've heard that, but I don't really believe there's a hidden treasure. Lamartine died before the Civil War. No one's found so much as a gold coin, and not for lack of trying."

"True." Wilma pointed to the vivid red spots on the cerulean dress. "Why the blood?"

PC wasn't entirely sure. It had seemed like the right thing at the time. "I… uh…"

"It's okay if you don't have an answer. The subconscious mind works in mysterious ways." Wilma moved on to the next student.

PC cleaned up her brushes and packed away her paints.

Wilma clapped her hands once. "Alright, everyone. You have fifteen minutes to finish and tidy up your tools."

Carefully handling her still-damp painting, PC left the classroom and stepped into the gallery. The owner, Drew Burlesconi, waved her over.

"Let me see!"

She was always a little bashful about showing her art to an expert. For her, it was a hobby, not a vocation. "Sure."

Careful not to touch the damp canvas, Drew gave it a once-over. "I like her. The impermanence of innocence. Wilma must have used the Lamartine today. Not too surprising. Next week is the re-enactment."

The detective nodded. *Was that what the blood spatter meant? Even though the woman wasn't involved, she still faced fallout from the conflict.* She didn't want to think that hard on a Saturday afternoon.

Drew looked up from the painting. "Speaking of which. Are we going to meet up for breakfast first, or just go there and take our chances with churros and funnel cake?"

PC set her painting on the counter. "I vote for City Café."

"Good plan. Were you able to get that wheelchair for Rose?"

PC huffed and rolled her eyes. "I told Mama she has gone to the Battle of Mirabella Creek re-enactment every single year since 1982. She could skip it this once—how different is it going to be? But she wants to see Terry re-enacting." PC sighed. "Fortunately, Dr. Thompson's office was able to get me a loaner—I just have to go pick it up."

"I think it's sweet that your mom has a boyfriend. Anyway, the last thing she needs is for that hip replacement to fail, so I'll volunteer to push her around."

PC laughed. "I'm going to hold you to that." She regarded her painting for a moment while she chose her words. "There's something else I have to do. I'm… um… I'm renting out a room in my house, and I have to go give my boarder her keys."

"Oh?" Drew cocked his head.

"Yeah. I had thought I'd be going back to Houston by now, but it looks like I'll be here a while longer—Mama's hip has had some setbacks. My neighbor's niece needed a place to stay—she's a college student."

His lips hinted at a smile. "Sounds like a win-win."

"I hope so."

The second Saturday in April was splendid and cool. PC's FlitBit showed 9:59 AM and Drew, Rose, PC, and her brother, Rocky, waited for the action to start. PC suspected that the aroma of cinnamon, sugar, and hot oil that hung in the air was not part of the original incursion. Today, the smell of barbecue was advancing along its flank from the south, aided by bursts of popping kettle corn artillery.

Hooves rumbled across the prairie like thunder as a small contingent of 1830s Mexican cavalry galloped up to the creek and halted. A knot of townsfolk, armed with farm implements and rifles, barred their way on the other side of the water—just like in the picture from the painting class last week. PC glanced over her shoulder, looking for the woman with the ash pail. Instead, a man with a rack of soft pretzels stood where she should have been.

The lead cavalryman drew his saber and slashed the air. "*Apártense!*"

"No! We will not move!" PC recognized the voice of the shouting man as Jim Hargraves, owner of the City Café. She wouldn't have known him in his settler garb.

The officer spurred his horse forward, but it balked at going into the water. A flintlock rifle fired, and the horse twisted and bucked, dropping the rider into the creek before bolting toward the horse trailers.

Rose giggled, and Rocky tried to shush her.

With shouts of "Remember Goliad!" and "Remember the Alamo!" more muskets fired, and PC could hardly make out the re-enactors through the gunpowder haze. Burned black powder, acrid and skunky, obliterated the comforting smells of food. PC's nose wrinkled.

The rest of the cavalry turned tail and fled, the soggy ex-rider scrambling up the creek bank and limping after them. A loud cheer erupted from the defenders, and the audience applauded.

A woman in a light brown settler's dress with a white apron and an oversized bonnet stepped onto the battlefield. Her wireless mic squealed as she turned it on.

"Sorry 'bout that! As many of you know, I'm Dinah Mae Brown, president of the Mirabella County Historical Society. We are so grateful for your support. Please make sure to—"

"Somebody call an ambulance! Roger Haney's been shot!"

Chapter 2

PC RAN DOWN to the battlefield where a distraught Jim Hargraves was trying to assist a fallen man. A glance told her it was too late for an ambulance. But she grabbed her phone from her back pocket and called, anyway.

"9-1-1. What's your emergency?"

"There's been an accident at the re-enactment. A man's been shot."

"That's at the State Park, ma'am?"

"Yes."

While she waited on the line with the operator until Possumwood PD showed up, she noted a large bruise on Roger's lower left arm. Fight? Fall? Freak accident?

Relief washed over PC when she saw the officer approaching the battlefield. Hiro Tran had been the first to befriend her when she came back to town and stepped right into a murder investigation.

"What happened?" Tran snapped on blue nitrile gloves.

"I don't know." Jim Hargraves' voice was so soft PC could barely hear him. "We did the same thing we've done for the past eight years. No one was supposed to use live ammo. How could this have gone so wrong?"

Tran abandoned his attempts at first aid. Even if he could get the victim's heart re-started, there was a musket ball-sized hole in it. He pulled out an emergency foil blanket from a little pouch on his belt and covered the face and upper body of the dead man, tucking the edges under the corpse so the flimsy sheet didn't fly away at the first breath of wind.

PC kneeled next to Hargraves. "I know this is hard, Jim. But we really need to ask while it's fresh in your mind. Could you start from the beginning? Tell us what happened as soon as you arrived this morning."

Technically, she didn't have the authority to question a witness, since she was a retired homicide detective. But she had worked a case last month as a contractor, and if it made Tran's life easier, she was sure he wouldn't object. There were only about fifteen personnel in the Possumwood Police Department, and none of them were trained detectives.

"I'll just record this, if you don't mind, Mr. Hargraves?" Tran held out his phone.

Hargraves' head bobbed. "Well…"

A siren wailed in the distance, and he looked up hopefully. "I picked Roger up this morning about seven. We had coffee at the Café and rolled up here a little before eight. I almost took him back home because he was having a terrible headache. I gave him a couple of the ibuprofen I keep in my glove box. He insisted on staying. We had a run-through at 8:30, then everybody got their kit on while they opened the gates and the spectators started coming in."

Tran recorded while PC continued with the questions. "Is there anybody new acting this year?"

Hargraves shook his head while he gnawed the inside of his cheek. "No. The newest person is Stan Zimmerman, and this is his fourth year."

"Biersal Brew Pub owner Stan Zimmerman?"

"Yeah."

"Who'll have a list of all the re-enactors?"

"Tom Wharton. He's the director."

The sirens were close now. PC looked up to see red and blue strobes bouncing off cars in the parking lot. A police cruiser and the official Tahoe of the police chief accompanied the ambulance. She turned back to the witness.

"Jim, did you see anything strange? Was anybody acting unusual?"

He stared morosely at Roger Haney's foot. "Now that you mention it. Truman Parker was fit to be tied when he got here. And Terry Gillespie was late—he missed half of the practice."

Over her shoulder, PC could hear the officers, one male, one female, clearing the crowd. The paramedics' gurney rattled over the uneven ground.

Tran interjected. "Alright, Mr. Hargraves. I think that'll be all for now. Would you mind coming by the station this afternoon so we can talk some more?"

"I guess I can."

Tran put his phone away. "The Medical Examiner is on the way, so we're going to have to ask everyone to leave while we're doing the investigation. We'll get the list of the actors from the director."

The female officer—Erin Sanchez—was putting up crime scene tape.

PC's knees crackled like Rice Krispies when she stood up. "Come on, Jim. Do you want to ride home with us? The Café's on the way to Mama's house."

"Thanks, but I'll be okay." He brushed off his pants and shuffled back toward the staging area.

The EMTs checked for vitals, officially declared Roger Haney dead, and left.

It's well past time to get Mama home. And Rocky. PC spotted them in the crowd and started in their direction.

A male voice came from her left. "Why am I not surprised to find you in the middle of this?"

"Good morning, Chief."

The Possumwood PD top cop scowled at her. "We hardly ever had homicides here. But since you've been back in town, Possumwood's become the murder capital of Mirabella County."

"Well." PC faked a smile. "It's nice to see you, too, Woody." She turned back toward her family.

"I'm sorry."

She nearly got whiplash from snapping her head around. "What?"

"This isn't your fault. Roger Haney was a good friend." He rubbed his forehead.

"I'm sorry for your loss." She said it automatically. Too many years of having to knock on doors in the middle of the night to make tragic notifications.

"Thanks. This has to have been an accident. He was a retired civil engineer who was really into history. Didn't have an enemy in the world."

"I'm sure he was a great guy." She patted his arm. "If you need any help on this one, you've got my number. I've got to get Mama out of the sun. I'm sorry about your friend."

This time, she made it all the way back to her family and Drew. Still in his 1836 garb, Terry Gillespie stood next to Rose, holding her hand.

Drew blotted his forehead with a handkerchief. "So, what happened?"

"I don't know much more than you do." PC ran a hand through her short salt and pepper hair. "Somebody used a live round, and Roger Haney got shot."

"Nobody is that careless. Not in our group." Terry's eyes blazed.

PC studied him for a moment. "You think it was intentional? Anybody can make a mistake."

Terry patted the powder horn slung at his hip. "You've never used a muzzle loader, have you?"

PC had gone to the firing range often enough to keep her firearms qualification. But not more than that. "No. I can't say that I have."

"Let me step you through it."

PC dipped her head toward Rose. "Can we go somewhere shadier?"

"Of course."

Terry led them to an immense live oak tree. PC doubted if she, Rocky, and Drew all held hands, they could make the circumference of it. He pulled his flintlock out of its case and rested the butt on the ground so that the barrel pointed skyward.

PC was distracted by the sight of a hearse pulling up and three men getting out, one of whom she recognized as Dr. Mack, the Medical Examiner.

Terry cleared his throat. "Now. The first thing you do is pour a little scoop of powder down its gullet." He patted the cow's horn sealed at the large end and stoppered at the narrow end that dangled from a leather thong just above his waist. "Then you take a patch of oiled fabric and put it over the hole. Put the musket ball on top of that, dead center, and push it and the patch into the barrel."

Drew leaned on the handles of Rose's wheelchair. "Must be fun on a windy day."

Terry snorted. "Most of us make a paper cartridge, so the powder is already measured. If you were using a ball, it would go in there, too. Plain cartridge or patch and ball. Either way, that's where your ramrod comes in—you have to shove it all the way down the barrel. Then you fill the flash pan, but that doesn't matter at this point. Do you see what I'm saying?"

"Could someone have accidentally brought a cartridge from home with a ball in it?" PC's brows knitted.

"Anybody would absolutely know whether their gun was loaded— you don't leave powder in the barrel, because it rusts if you do. Besides, there's a safety inspection before we take the field. And live ammo is strictly banned from any performance."

Drew shifted his weight toward PC. "That certainly makes an accident seem less likely."

She glanced at him before turning her head back to Terry. "But somebody could, theoretically, have a cartridge with the musket ball inside hidden in their pocket."

Terry stroked his chin. "I suppose they could."

PC wiped the sweat before it dripped into her eyes. "I think we should get out of the heat. Do you need a ride, Terry?"

He patted his pants pockets and then shook his head. "Had to check to make sure they were in my pocket. I was late this morning because I couldn't find my dang car keys. I'll come by and see you in a little bit, Rose." He kissed the top of her head and turned toward the re-enactor parking.

He hadn't gotten very far when Woody and Officer Sanchez stopped him.

"Mr. Gillespie?" Woody asked, artificially pleasant. "Would you mind coming down to the station with us? We'd like to ask you some questions."

Chapter 3

"Terry?" Rose called out, half rising from her wheelchair. "Why do the po-lice want to talk to you?"

"It's okay, Mama." PC put her hand on her mother's shoulder. "Let me just go over there and see what's going on."

She walked as fast as she could without coming across as aggressive. At least, that's what she hoped.

"Wh-what's this about?" Terry swallowed hard.

Woody held up a plastic evidence bag. "When the boys from the funeral home lifted the body, we found this."

Inside the bag was a thumb-sized bright orange glob of something PC couldn't identify. But Terry's eyes widened.

"I don't understand. I didn't even bring any shot with me." He shook his head, and his voice pitched upward. "We're not allowed. I didn't…"

"Excuse me." PC put a comforting hand on Terry's shoulder, but faced Woody. "What exactly did you find?"

He handed the bag over. "This is the musket ball that killed Roger Haney."

PC moved the object around in the bag so she could get a better look. It appeared as if someone had taken a bit of orange-yellow modeling clay and rolled it on the ground to pick up some dirt while they were making it into a ball, then thrown it at a wall as hard as they could.

About three quarters of it had flattened into a disk, while the very back of it was still round.

She handed the bag back. "And what makes you think it's Terry's?"

"Three different people identified it as his. Now you're probably already aware of this, since he's been keepin' company with your mama. And how is your mama, by the way?"

"She's fine. Hip's going well." PC breathed deeply and forced her breath out slowly to dissipate her frustration. His southern charm felt more like southern smarm.

"Good. Glad to hear it. As I was sayin', Terry's a big environmentalist. He adds a little bit of pigment to the molten lead when he makes his bullets so that he can make sure he gets all of it picked up when they go shootin.'"

"I'm sure any of those re-enactors who make their own shot could have done that."

Terry drooped. "I have a secret formula. Took me a lot of experimenting to get it just the way I wanted it. But I didn't do this! I swear!"

"Jim Hargraves told us you and Roger had words yesterday. And you threatened him." Woody said.

"I didn't kill him!"

PC turned back to Terry. "Do you have a lawyer?"

He stared at the grass. "No."

Her eyes softened. "Terry?"

He looked up. She watched his Adam's apple bob. Terry possibly had motive, and he definitely had means and opportunity. This crime was clearly premeditated, but if he'd gone to the effort to sneak a live round into the re-enactment, he wouldn't have been stupid enough to use one that was so easily identifiable. Probability of him being framed was 99.999%.

"I believe you. I'm going to call my Uncle Raymond to meet you at the station, okay? Don't say anything until he gets there."

Terry nodded.

Woody gestured toward the parking lot. "Come on, Mr. Gillespie. Let's go."

PC hurried back to her mother, Rocky, and Drew.

"Why are they arresting Terry?" Rose panted, struggling to catch her breath.

"Mama, get a hold of yourself. Everything's going to be okay." PC cut her eyes to the walkway. Drew began to push Rose's wheelchair. "They're not arresting him. Just taking him in for questioning. There's some circumstantial evidence that Terry is the one that shot Mr. Haney—"

"What?" Rose almost fell out of her chair.

"Calm down. I don't think he did it, but it doesn't look too good for him right now. I want you to call Uncle Raymond and tell him to meet Terry at the police station."

Rose got her phone out of her bag, but her hands were shaking so hard it was difficult for her to scroll through her contacts.

PC gently took the phone. "Here. Let me do it." She found her uncle's number and tapped it before handing the device back to her mother.

"Ray?… Fine. No, it's not about that. Terry Gillespie has just been taken downtown for questioning. Elwood Wilson thinks he shot Roger Haney!… Yes, here at the re-enactment… No… No… Just now… Thank you so much! Love you… Bye."

Once they got to the car, Rocky helped Rose into her seat while Drew packed the wheelchair into the cargo area. PC supervised the stowing operation.

Drew pushed the button to close the liftgate. "How much trouble do you think Terry's in?"

"Well, you've experienced first-hand how when Woody gets a bee in his bonnet, he won't let it out. But Terry'd have to be dumber than a bag of wet hair to have brought one of his special dyed bullets to kill Roger Haney. Guess at least some measure of trouble depends on whether the DA is of the get-to-the-truth or get-a-conviction mindset."

Drew shrugged. "I don't run in the same circles as Travis Bailey, but he seems reasonable, underneath all the bluster."

"How well did you know Roger Haney?"

"I've met him once or twice at Historical Society functions, but I wouldn't say we were friends."

"I see." PC fidgeted with her key fob. "I need to run Mama home. But I plan to poke around and see what I can find out. It was, uh, an interesting morning."

"You got that right. Keep me posted on what you find out. See you Wednesday?"

"Wild horses couldn't drag me away from our weekly darts challenge."

Drew grinned as he turned and headed to his car. PC watched him for a moment, then slid into the driver's seat. Rocky and Rose were already buckled in.

"Okay." PC shifted the car into drive. "Were either of you close to Roger Haney? Or have any idea what he and Terry might have gotten into a fight about yesterday?"

Rocky piped up from the back seat. "I only met him the one time—"

He stopped himself, and PC could see him in the rearview mirror, looking at Rose's headrest. She stared out the window, gnawing on her thumbnail.

"Mama?"

Rose sighed heavily. "I've known Roger since high school. His wife passed not too long after he retired, so he spends—spent—a lot of time volunteerin' at the historical society and the library. He's not, well, I don't think he was a bad sort, just very, very persistent. Always had his nose in a book. He wasn't snooty, so much as just plain oblivious."

"Oblivious to what?" PC pulled out onto the highway.

"Pretty much everything. You were at the feed store yesterday, and Rocky was home on his lunch break. Roger... came to the house. He had a big ole bouquet of flowers and a bottle of wine. It was obvious what he had in mind. I told him I was flattered, but I wasn't interested. He wouldn't take no for an answer. He's been calling me every day for the past week. After the first time, I quit answerin'. Guess he thought he had to step it up in person to get anywhere."

Rocky leaned forward to peer through the gap between the front seats. "I had to come out and tell him to git."

"And then?"

Rose crossed her hands in her lap, then re-crossed them. "I didn't want to trouble you while you were out, so I ordered two plates of chicken fried steak from the City Café for Rocky and me, and Jim Hargraves said he'd bring it over. He was just gettin' out of the van when Terry came down the sidewalk. He saw Roger with the flowers and Jim with the food, and he got all bowed up. His face got so dark red, I thought his head was like to explode."

County Road 27 turned into Justice Avenue, and PC stopped at a light. "Go on."

"Terry was in a state. That's for sure. He asked Roger just what it was he thought he was doin', and Roger said 'What does it look like?' And Terry came chargin' over, saying, 'Stay away from Rose! She's told you over and over she isn't interested. Quit bothering her—what are you, some kind of stalker?' Well, that put Roger's back right up, and he went after Terry. Jim got a hold of Roger and Rocky got a hold of Terry and kept 'em apart. I thought Jim had talked sense into both of 'em, 'cuz they both left. Although Roger did say somethin' passing strange."

"And what was that?"

Rocky butted in. "'This time next week, you'll wish you had chosen me.' Then he laughed."

PC slowed for a right turn. "Sounds like he either meant to do Terry harm, or thought he was coming into some money."

Rose shook her head. "I had no idea what to make of it. Anyway, I was so upset that I couldn't eat. Rocky polished off both plates."

PC eyed her brother in the mirror. "No wonder you didn't want dinner."

"Hey! Aren't we goin' to the police station?" Rose cried as PC passed the turning.

"Mama, the last thing you need is to go sit around on a hard plastic chair at Possumwood PD. I'm taking you and Rocky home."

"But—"

"Mama! There's *nothing* you can do. Uncle Raymond will take care of it. He'll bring Terry home or take him to pick up his car. Whatever he needs. You aren't going to do anybody any good if your blood pressure goes through the roof, or you pop your hip out of the socket again."

They rode the rest of the way down Travis Lane in silence. PC tapped absently on the steering wheel. Anger and fear can make people do very stupid things.

Perhaps Terry had a motive, after all.

Chapter 4

PC WENT AHEAD to open doors while Rocky helped their mother out of PC's SUV. No point in lugging in the wheelchair—Rose could walk from the driveway to the house on Rocky's arm well enough.

"I wish y'all wouldn't treat me like an invalid," Rose grumbled.

PC unlocked the door and held it open. "Now Mama, the doctor said take it easy on that hip for thirty days after your procedure. It's only been eight. I know you're used to doing for yourself, but this is all temporary, *if* you do as Dr. Thompson told you."

Rose grunted as she plopped into her recliner and then leaned back.

Rocky looked up from his search for the TV remote. "You okay, Mama?"

"Yes."

PC rubbed her temple. "You want something to drink? Iced tea? Water?"

"Well, if you're goin' to the kitchen anyway, I could use a glass of tea."

Rocky clicked the TV on. "Can you bring me some, too?"

"Of course." That rankled PC. Rocky was perfectly capable of getting his own tea, and Rose's tea as well. But she should be grateful, she supposed, that it was only tea he was drinking lately. He'd been good about going to his AA meetings, and he'd been sober for over a hundred days now—Rose had taken him and PC to Zeno's for pizza to celebrate on Wednesday. Besides, if it keeps him on the wagon, she told herself, it's just as easy to pour two glasses as it is one.

Now. What about Terry Gillespie?

She pulled two big red plastic tumblers from the cupboard and filled them with ice, then tea from a pitcher in the fridge. As she turned back toward the living room, her heart skipped a beat.

Dammit, Guinevere. Not today.

Through the kitchen window, she saw that the gate to the pen was ajar. Arthur, the one-eyed jack, paced around the enclosure. He stopped and let out a loud *haw-haw-haw-heeeeeeee!* There was no sign of either Gwen, the beige donkey, or Hazel the goat.

PC hurried into the living room and set the glasses down on the coffee table. "I've got to go find Gwen—she's opened the gate again."

The detective grabbed her car keys and rushed out the door before either her mother or brother could respond.

Better grab halters and some feed.

Hazel was grazing on the north side of the house, near the ditch along Travis Street. PC whistled to her. The goat flicked a droopy ear, but otherwise ignored her.

A bucket with a little feed rattling in it, however, got Hazel's full attention, and she pogoed her way back to the pen at full speed. Even though the goat only had three legs, she was both strong and fast, and PC knew better than to attempt to grab her. That wouldn't end well for anybody.

Once Hazel was safely back inside the pen, PC gave her and Arthur each a handful of feed, making sure to stay on Arthur's right side so he could see her. She scratched the donkey's neck.

"Don't worry. I bet Gwennie's looking for roses. I know just where to go."

She took the bucket and a halter and made double sure the gate was fully latched before she jogged to her SUV. As long as there was food, Arthur, Hazel, and the chickens were happy homebodies, but Guinevere was an eager escapologist, and PC was going to have to do a better job of thwarting her wanderlust.

She hit pay dirt the first place she looked. Gwen didn't appear to have been at Truman Parker's first-prize-at-the-county-fair rose bushes for long. They were still bushing out from the hard pruning he'd given them back in February. PC pulled over and opened the liftgate. Gwen's beige radar dish ears swiveled toward the car.

PC got the feed and the halter, then gave the bucket a good shake. Gwen gave a little buck and a big fart before she trotted up to the SUV.

Keepin' it classy, huh, Gwen?

The front door to the Parker's house opened, and Truman, dressed in a rust-colored terry robe, leaned against the frame.

"I'm so sorry, Mr. Parker. Gwen's figured out how to open the new latch I put on the gate."

He snorted, or perhaps it was a resigned laugh. "What else is gonna go wrong today, huh?"

That's right. Jim Hargraves said Truman was really upset when he came to the rehearsal this morning.

Gwen had almost finished the small amount of pellets in the bucket, so PC put the rope around her neck and got ready to slip on the halter.

"Terrible shame about Roger Haney, isn't it?"

"Yeah. Somethin' was goin' on with him lately. He was actin' real weird."

Gwen came up for air, and PC slid the noseband over her muzzle and buckled the halter. "Really? How so?"

"He's been spending a lot of time in the library and the courthouse, looking at old property records. Got real jumpy and defensive if anybody asked what he was doin."

"Mama said he was really into history."

"Yeah, but not like this. He usually couldn't stop flappin' his gums about it."

"Oh. I thought since you were doing the re-enactment, you were a history buff as well."

Parker laughed. "I *have* horses. The cavalry *needs* horses. Dinah Mae is my wife's cousin's sister-in-law. I was just a cavalryman. Same as always." His head bobbled like one of those old dashboard hula girls. "That's where the day got off to a bad start. That Bill Montoya... some people watch a video on the internet, and suddenly they're an expert."

Gwen shoved the empty feed bucket with her muzzle.

Not now, Guinevere. PC let the donkey drop her nose to graze.

Bill sometimes came to play darts on Wednesday nights, but PC didn't know him well. "Doesn't he have the car dealership off 720? What did he do?"

"Yeah. Ford House." Parker crossed his arms. "He rides a horse exactly one time per year, at the re-enactment. But at least he does come to help load up the trailer in the morning. Anyway, he watched some video on how a Mexican gaucho saddle is rigged, so he went and bought the parts off eBay. First of all, Cocoa is the only horse I have that will pack Bill around, and that contraption did not fit him. Second, the Mexican cavalry used the Spanish-style saddles with no horn—they were expecting to run infantry through with a saber, not rope cattle. I told him no, he wasn't putting that thing on my horse, and he pestered me about it the whole way from my barn to the parking lot. I had to get Tom Wharton to veto his nonsense."

PC remembered Wharton. He'd been her American History teacher, fresh out of college, when she was a junior in high school. Dinosaurs still roamed the Earth then. He was basketball player height and built like a tank. Half the girls had crushes on him.

She scratched Gwen's mohawk mane. "I thought you said Cocoa was a packer? He gave Bill a bath once the shooting started."

Parker grinned. "That's because he got on Mingo by accident. He looks very similar to Cocoa, but he's only five, and pretty green. I will admit, I got a lot of satisfaction when he dumped Bill in the creek."

PC knew she shouldn't laugh, but she couldn't entirely squelch it, either. It took her a moment to regain control. "You had a different vantage point from where we were in the audience. Did you notice anything strange or unusual once the shooting started?"

"No. Once they started popping those blanks, the smoke was so thick I could barely see anything. Fog of war and all that."

PC started to gather the lead rope, pulling Guinevere in closer to her. She'd have to lead the donkey home, then come back for her vehicle.

"Although, now that you mention it, right after the dry run, Roger Haney and Jim Hargraves were having words. Which is kinda strange, because those two are usually thick as thieves. Now, I might have misunderstood, because it was noisy, but I was sure I heard Jim say, 'No, I'm not gonna help you. You'll get us *both* killed.' Then Roger stormed off."

Chapter 5

"REALLY. WONDER WHAT he meant by that?" PC tugged on Guinevere's lead. "I am so sorry that Gwen's come for your roses again, Mr. Parker."

"You can take a length of chain and fasten it around the post and gate with a double-ended snap. Had some Houdinis in my time, but never one yet that could work a snap. But don't cheap out—make sure you get the heavy-duty kind."

"I'll have to try that. Be back for my car soon. Hope the rest of your day is better."

Parker gave a half-hearted nod. "Thanks. And while you're at the hardware store, you can ask Tim Kowalski what he meant by telling Roger he ought to call the police on him." He stepped back inside and shut the door.

"Mama, you want me to order something to eat?" PC's stomach gurgled loudly.

The City Café did not serve dinner. But they did serve lunch for another half an hour.

"I don't really feel like eating."

Rocky paused his TV show. "You need to keep your strength up."

PC silently agreed. She remembered how thin and frail her mother had become forty years ago, when PC and Rocky's father had been murdered. Rose had been on the verge of being hospitalized. Her sisters, Lily and Camelia, had to step in and get her back on her feet.

When PC first returned to Possumwood, she had been given her father's murder book, and she studied it every night, hoping to find some clue to bring the killer to justice. But mostly, it just felt like picking scabs and getting fresh blood from an old wound.

"He's right, Mama. Why don't you let me get you something from the City Café?"

"I guess, if they still have some soup of the day left."

Rocky licked his lips. "I've got a craving for a cheeseburger. And curly fries."

"Okay. We'll split the tab. I'll go call it in."

He un-paused the TV, and PC moved into the kitchen with her cell phone.

"City Café."

"Hey, Winnie. PC Donovan. How's Jim doing?"

Winnie Hargraves sighed. "He's really taking this hard. Still at the state park, helping the police look for clues. Or evidence or some such."

"I'm really sorry for your loss."

"Thank you. Roger was like a member of the family. How's your mama doin'?"

"She's okay. Ornery as all get out, but you already knew that."

Winnie laughed softly. "I appreciate you asking after Jim…"

PC took the hint. "Yeah. I, um, I'd also like to make an order for takeout. Or delivery, if you have time."

"Sure. What can I get for you?"

"What soup do you have?"

"Chicken and dumplings."

"Good. Bowl of that, cheeseburger with curly fries, and grilled cheese with a side salad."

"What about dessert? I made chocolate chiffon pie today."

"Ow! You're twisting my arm. Let's have three pieces of that, too. Will you be able to deliver it, or should I come and pick it up?"

"I can bring it. Seems like a lot of folks filled up on turkey legs and churros at the re-enactment—we're pretty slow today."

Thirty minutes later, the white City Café van pulled up in front of Rose's house. PC's terrier mix, Cordite, stirred himself from the couch and barked.

PC tapped Rocky on the shoulder. "Come on."

"Do you really need—"

Her death stare cut him short.

"Fine."

They walked out to meet Winnie.

PC handed the plastic bag of hot lunches to her brother. "I'll be there in a minute." She waited until the screen door banged behind him. "Winnie, I know this is a difficult time. But I want to find out who killed Roger, too. Probably almost as bad as Jim does. And I really need your help."

"My help? I'm not sure what I can do, but I'll try. Jim isn't going to rest until Roger's killer is brought to justice."

PC nodded. "Did Jim ever talk about Terry Gillespie and Roger?"

"Lord have mercy. Those two?"

"What about them?"

"Jim said there was nearly a donnybrook yesterday. Apparently, Roger came courtin' Rose, and Terry was none too pleased that he won't give up this lost cause." Winnie sighed and shuffled her feet. "Roger's been carrying a torch for your mama since they were in high school. Broke his heart when she married Trey. Roger thought he might have a chance when he... died. But Rose, I'm not sure she's over your daddy even now. Even though Roger eventually married Sonia Wagner, and they had a good life together, I don't think he ever stopped pining after your mama. I would say he was generally sane in most other matters, just not when it came to Rose Donovan."

"That's so sad that he was never able to move on. I feel bad for his wife."

Winnie laid her hand on her chest. "As that old saying goes, the heart wants what the heart wants."

PC winced. "It must have been hard for him to see her with Terry, now that he was single again and thought she was, too."

"That ate at him like acid. He got really obsessed with some research project he was doing. Jim couldn't even get him to go fishin' at the lake. I believe Roger thought he had some scheme to win Rose's heart once and for all."

"But he didn't say what it was?"

Winnie frowned. "No. Jim said Roger had started spending all day in either the library or the courthouse. Then, all of a sudden, he just stopped. Would you believe he wanted Jim to help him break into Ada Dotson's house? That's a suicide mission if ever there was one."

PC's head involuntarily jerked in surprise. "The liquor store owner?"

"Yeah. Ada's armed to the teeth—got weapons hidden everywhere. Did you know she was a Marine at the tail end of Viet Nam? I think she was in the service twenty years, all told."

"I didn't, but it doesn't surprise me." The last time PC had seen her, Ada had been standing on her front porch, smoking a cigar. "What was it Roger wanted there?"

"Jim told me Roger was itchin' to take some pictures of a paintin'."

"And he couldn't have just asked her?"

Winnie shrugged. "He wouldn't even tell Jim what painting or why."

The acrylics class last week. Maybe Roger had figured out the clues the Blue Lady was dropping. "Ada lives in a historic home. Does she, by chance, have a Lamartine painting in her house?"

"No idea. But there's several at the Quenton Plantation." She chuckled. "Every time we go there, Jim thinks he's going to solve the clues and find the treasure. Then he forgets about it by the time we get home."

"People have been searching for that almost two hundred years. Personally, I think it's just a story." PC ran a finger down her chin. "Did Roger believe in the hidden treasure? Could that have been what he was looking for?"

Winnie shrugged. "Could be. He got awful tight-lipped about whatever he was up to. That man used to come over for dinner at least once a week, and between malt whiskey and pecan pie, would tell you every thought in his head. Thursday night was the first time I've seen him since that fella got kilt on the Azalea Trail last month. Roger must have discovered internet shoppin' or somethin', 'cause he was flashier than a rat with a gold tooth in that get-up he was wearing."

"Why online shopping?"

Winnie wiped her face with her apron. "Roger didn't have a car. Rode his bike or got a ride everywhere."

"And he didn't give you any clue about his plans?" PC rubbed her arm.

"Other than he was cock-sure it would work, no."

"Winnie, where are my manners? Would you like to come inside for a glass of tea and visit with Mama?"

"I'd love to, hon, but I can't right now. I've got to get back to the restaurant and finish closin'."

"Thank you so much. I'm sure Mama wishes she could give you both a big hug."

PC waved as the van pulled away, then went inside to eat her lunch.

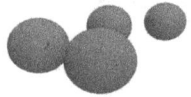

Justice Hardware was exactly the sort of over-stuffed store that one often found out in the country. And PC loved it. In front of the store, they had spring vegetables and bedding plants, along with a small assortment of fruit trees.

Just inside, a rescue group tended a doggie playpen full of puppies. Cordite would be mad, smelling other canines on PC's clothes, but she couldn't resist.

"What kind of dogs are these?" she asked a teenager in a bright blue shirt with a Just Paws logo.

"They're purebred mongrels."

PC chuckled. The herd of puppies stampeded toward the gate.

The volunteer grinned. "There's three different litters in there. The fluffy ones are a shepherd mix, the white and brown ones are a beagle cross, and the rest, well, we know the mom was a lab."

"My dog would never forgive me if I brought home a puppy." She leaned over and put her hand against the mesh and plump little doggos waddled over to greet her. *I need a puppy like I need a hole in my head.* But she still picked up a card from the folding table near the pen.

To her right were rows of shelves holding bins of various hardware store staples—nails, screws, toilet tank repair kits, and so on. That's where she'd find brass snaps and chains.

She turned to the left.

Greeting cards. Fridge magnets. Mega-muffin tins. Canning supplies. Tablecloths. Pet supplies.

She found a bottle of dog shampoo that smelled like vanilla and lavender and tucked it under her arm. PC located the fastener aisle and started going through a bin of brass double-ended snaps.

"Is there anything I can help you find, Miss?"

PC looked up to see a very fit, fortyish man in a Justice Hardware uniform standing at the front of the aisle. She recognized him as Tim Kowalski, the store's owner.

"Sure. I'm looking for a couple feet of chain and a double-ended snap to keep my mom's sneaky donkey from opening the gate. These snaps seem to be all mixed up."

He frowned and strode over to the bin. Once he looked inside, his frown deepened into a scowl. "I'll have to get someone to clean that up." Tim dug around for a few moments before producing a large brass snap. "Aha! Here you go. Let's go cut you some chain. How much do you want? Two feet or three?"

"What does chain cost?" She imagined $30 or $40.

"You should be fine with quarter inch—that's…" He scrunched up his face, trying to remember. "I think $3.00 per foot."

That's a relief! At least something's gone right today. "Three feet should be more than enough. Say, weren't you one of the re-enactors this morning?"

Tim's shoulders stiffened. "Yes, I was. Why do you ask?"

"I thought it was terrible what happened to Roger Haney. That's all. He was an old friend of my mother's."

Tim's eyes narrowed. "Your mother has a sneaky donkey, you say? The only one in town that fits that description is Rose Donovan. She's a nice lady, but she really should choose better friends."

Chapter 6

PC BRISTLED. TIM Kowalski, who had been known to date married women, was one to talk about the quality of Rose's friends. "What do you mean by that?"

He looked over his shoulder and leaned towards her. "Look, I don't want to make a big deal out of it. I know you're with the po-lice, but I'm not interested in filing a report, okay? On Wednesday, I caught Roger trying to shoplift a pipe locator. I didn't press charges, but I told him not to come back in my store. Roger's not a bad guy, but he is… peculiar. Anyway, Friday morning, when I was out for my run, I saw him poking around in the mayor's back yard. He saw me and ran off. I called Phineas and told him about it when I got home."

"And what did he say?"

Kowalski shrugged. "He said his dog barked a little earlier than usual, and he thought it needed to go to the bathroom, so he let it out in the back yard, but Phineas didn't notice anybody out there."

"Maybe it wasn't you Roger was running from."

"Yeah. That dog…"

"I've heard him called a Chupacabra."

Kowalski gave a snort of laughter and straightened back up. "What is it? A showkaqueeny something."

"I'm not even going to try to pronounce that. The mayor told us he was a Mexican Hairless. He's called Anubis, if I remember correctly."

"I can believe that."

Kowalski stopped at the spools of by-the-foot chain and uncoiled a length of one of the lighter weight ones. PC watched while he measured out three feet, then cut it.

"There you go. Anything else I can help you with?"

"You wouldn't happen to have any idea, or even a good guess, as to what Roger Haney wanted with a pipe locator, would you?"

"No. I didn't ask him. But it's got lots of different modes. You can find wires, plastic pipe, fiber optic cable—all of that with it."

"What about gold?"

Kowalski's forehead wrinkled. "Not sure about that, though. Probably better off with a standard metal detector."

"Do you carry metal detectors?"

"No. But I can order one for you."

"No, that's okay. Thank you, Mr. Kowalski. I appreciate your help."

He handed her a ticket for the chain. "Brenda'll take care of you at the register."

PC was almost to the end of the aisle when he called out. "Oh, miss, uh, is it Donovan?"

"Yes?"

"Stan Zimmerman might have an idea what Roger was up to. The two of them were having a discussion this morning after the dry run. They stood over with the horses, like they didn't want anybody to overhear."

"Interesting. Thanks!"

PC took the long way home. She drove by Possumwood PD and saw her Uncle Raymond's car parked out front. She hoped that was good. Next up, Phineas Scott's house. PC wanted to see if there was anything obvious from the road that might cause Roger Haney to investigate. Hopefully, Gwen wouldn't go on another excursion while PC was looking around.

She pulled into the utility easement behind the mayor's house and got out of her car. An unpruned Texas sage bush flourished near the back gate of the chain-link fence, magenta flowers crowding out the velvety silver leaves. Mama always said that the sage bloomed right before a rain. If that was true, a gully washer must be on the way, what with that mass of flowers. Inside the gate, a metal arbor held up an ancient star jasmine vine, thick as PC's wrist. The sweet perfume wafting off the wall of white flowers made her slightly light-headed.

Closer to the house, a gazebo covered a collection of cushioned wicker chairs underneath a ceiling fan with blades shaped like banana leaves. A brick-edged pond with a fountain at one end lay between the gazebo and the home, spanned by the bright red arch of a Japanese bridge. An outdoor kitchen, with a fireplace and table that sat six, was on the deck next to the house. It had a roof, supported by brick pillars, but the only wall was where the cooking equipment was. It had its own botanical-inspired ceiling fan.

On the far side of the yard, near the garage, stood an old-fashioned stone well. A fluted concrete planter, filled with pink and white petunias, took up most of the wooden cover, which was held on with a heavy, rusty chain. *Rest easy, Lassie—Timmy's not getting in there.* The water bucket lay on its side next to the well, blue flowers in a tear-drop shaped bed, narrow end at the bucket as if they were spilling out of it. Closer to the fence and taking up a large portion of the northeast quarter of the property, was a thick, gnarled live oak so old that some of its heavy limbs rested on the ground. Could that be what Roger was looking for? Was there a hollow in the tree where something might be concealed?

She got back in her car, wanting to get home and secure the gate from the infamous sneaky donkey. It was getting close to feeding time, anyway, and she didn't want to inflict Guinevere and Arthur's punishing cacophony at her tardiness on the neighbors. She just had one more stop to make.

Five-thirty was a bit early for the Saturday crowd at the Biersal Brew Pub, and PC was counting on it not being too busy. She hoped at least one of the owners, Stanley and Kenneth, the Zimmerman twins, was there. Preferably Stan.

It would be cruel to Rocky to buy a six pack of their craft beer and keep it in Rose's refrigerator. She briefly thought of buying it, then taking it to Drew's, but reconsidered. The critters were guaranteed a late dinner if she did that. She'd get some of the house-made soft pretzels and a pint of their creamy cheddar dip to go. The Biersal was closed on Mondays, and she really didn't want to wait until she was there for her weekly darts game with Drew and a few other friends on Wednesday night.

The thought of him brought a smile to her lips. Then she shook herself out of her woolgathering—she'd almost clipped a parked car as she pulled into the Biersal's parking lot.

What are you, fifteen? She took a few deep breaths to de-fluster herself before going inside.

PC pulled open half of the double door, and the smells of hops and pizza enveloped her like a hug from an old friend. A handful of patrons loafed around the dart boards, half-empty beer pitchers adorning the small olive-green tables that floated like lily pads on the dark blue carpet.

Perfect.

The Biersal had a small kitchen where they made mostly quick foods, like sandwiches and pizza. But their breads. The house-made bread at the brew pub was famous among the town's ten-thousand residents, and communities beyond. It drew diners all the way from Houston. And Possumwood was not exactly on the beaten track. Visitors also came for camping, boating, and fishing at the lake in Mirabella Creek State Park, and of course, the Quenton Plantation Historical Park, with live re-enactors on the weekends. *Happily Ever Afters*, which locals just called 'the Afters,' was a popular wedding venue and bed & breakfast. Antiquers and collectors could check out *Vintage Glory Antiques*, *Sweet July Vintage Clothing*, or Drew's place, *The Best Little Art Gallery in Texas*. There was some type of fair or festival most months. All of those things attracted tourists, true, but no one was likely to wander into Possumwood unless they intended to be there. Many people planned weekends around the attractions and the famous Biersal bread.

PC smiled at the bartender. "Hey, Peggy. How are you? Do you have any pretzels left?"

"I'm excellent." Then she scanned the bar, brows knit. "It isn't Wednesday already, is it?"

"No, no. I just had a craving for some pretzels, and I thought I'd stop by. And I had a quick question for Stan Zimmerman, if he's around."

"There's pretzels in the oven—they should be out soon. Mr. S was here earlier, but I'm not sure if he's still here. I can call his office."

"That'd be great. Thanks, Peggy."

While she waited, PC scanned the room, looking for acquaintances. Instead, her eyes fell on a familiar face. How many times had she seen her, but never noticed?

Chapter 7

THE WOMAN WORE a crimson dress. While the high collar brushed her jawline, the vee neck plunged scandalously low, only kept from being obscene by a wide, scalloped lace edging. Her dark hair was pulled into a severe bun, but a few rogue tendrils curled daintily around her face.

PC had seen her every Wednesday night for the last two and a half months, and she only just now snapped to it. It was the style that caught her eye. After last week's acrylics workshop, she'd recognize Francois de Lamartine's painting style anywhere. The portrait hung at the end of the bar, decorating the wall near the door to the manager's office. PC walked over for a closer look.

A brass plaque on the frame read, 'Portrait of Hannah de Lamartine.' The woman was beautiful, with huge brown eyes and a pink rosebud of a mouth. She stood in a white-framed glass conservatory, with spring bursting behind her outside. A large potted fern arched gracefully to her right inside the sunroom.

But there was something else. Another Lamartine quirk. The same woman in blue who was in the picture of the Battle of Mirabella Creek stood in the left corner of the glass room, holding a cake on a red plate. A cardinal caught in mid-flap stretched its feet to a branch near the glass by the Blue Lady.

Who are you?

She got out her phone and snapped a few pictures of the painting.

"PC? I heard you were looking for me?"

She turned to find Stan Zimmerman grinning at her. "Hey, Stan. Is this painting a Lamartine original?"

"I believe so."

"Do you know anything about the Blue Lady?"

"I think she's in a lot of his paintings, but other than that, no. Is that what you wanted to see me about?"

PC stuffed her phone back into her pocket. "No. Sorry. I just hadn't remembered her being here. Could we go to your office?"

"I suppose."

She followed him down the short corridor. He pushed open a door with an *Employees Only* sign.

Everything about the office was medium: medium-sized, medium light, and medium quality furniture. PC thought she caught the scent of pipe tobacco, but wasn't sure if it was real, or just the candle in the corner of the room under the German cuckoo clock, which featured two men in lederhosen drinking beer.

Stan gestured to a fabric and steel chair. "Have a seat."

She sat. "Thanks."

"Now. What can I help you with?"

PC ran a hand through her hair. "Perhaps you've heard that Terry Gillespie's being questioned for the murder of Roger Haney. I'm not sure if they are going to charge him. But I don't think he did it."

Stan rested his jaw on his left hand, his elbow on the arm of the chair. "You've been working with the police, though. Won't they tell you?"

"That's the thing. Since Terry and my mother have a relationship, I'm sure they won't tell me anything. Uncle Raymond is with him, so maybe we'll get more information soon. For her sake, I'm trying to trace the last few days of Roger's life. Maybe I can find somebody else with a motive."

Stan nodded. When he spoke, his voice was deeper, more gravelly. "Kinda like one of those *Investigation Discovery* shows. I've known Terry a long time, and I can't believe he'd kill anyone, either. So, what brings you to me?"

"I heard that you and Roger were having an intense conversation this morning before the performance."

Stan leaned against the backrest of his chair and fiddled with a pen on his desk. "Yeah. It's true. He buttonholed me after the dry run." He slumped. "I sure wish he'd have told me what was going on."

"What did he tell you?"

"He wanted to borrow money. Swore he could pay me back in two weeks, three tops."

"How much did he want?"

"$10,000. I think Uncle Roger had the wrong idea about the amount of profit the Biersal makes. I've got two kids in college, and you wouldn't believe the insurance on the brewery."

PC leaned forward. "He was your uncle?"

"Technically, he is—was—our mother's cousin, but it was just easier calling him Uncle. Always a bit of an odd duck, and we didn't see that much of him, but he was a good guy."

"I am so sorry. My condolences."

Stan picked up the pen and started doodling on the desk pad. "I wish he would have told me what the money was for. When he was so secretive about it, I was worried he'd gotten hooked by some scam artist. You know, one of those Nigerian Prince emails or something? I was just trying to save him, and I got a little cross with him because he was being so uncooperative."

Nothing more awful than harsh words and never being able to make it up. Wish I had something to say that would make any difference. "Stan, again, I'm sorry for your loss. I'd never have intruded, if I'd realized."

"It's okay. If there is anything at all you can do to help find Uncle Roger's killer, Ken and I would be extremely grateful. He's at the funeral home now, making the arrangements for when the body is released."

PC stood up. "I will do everything I can to put the killer in a cage." She learned long ago never to promise a victim's family that they would catch the murderer. Sometimes it didn't happen. "I'll see myself out."

"Thank you. Oh, PC? Have the police already talked to Truman Parker? I thought he and Roger were going to come to blows during rehearsal."

Chapter 8

PC BLINKED. "I'm sorry? You said he and Truman Parker were fighting? What about?" *Parker failed to mention that to me when I spoke with him earlier.*

Stan shrugged. "No idea. But Truman was shaking a rope at Uncle Roger, and he said, 'I catch you doing that again, and I will skin you alive.' Sounds pretty threatening to me. If nobody's talked to him, they should get on it right away."

"Yes. I will definitely look into that."

PC was so distracted walking out of the manager's office that she almost forgot her pretzels.

Rocky held the white paper bag against his chest as if it were filled with diamonds.

PC froze him with a look. "There are six pretzels in there. Two each. I'm fixin' to feed the animals. My pretzels had better be in there when I get back."

He grinned at her.

"What's so funny?"

"You said 'fixin' to.' You're startin' to talk like a country girl again."

She held up her index and middle fingers. "Two pretzels."

I need to get home. So many reasons I left Possumwood the minute I finished high school.

Now that the graduate student, Felicity Campbell, was renting her house in Houston, PC didn't have to go every week to check on the place. On her trips into Houston, she stopped at her favorite restaurants and visited her friends. The longer she stayed in Possumwood, the more she might fade out of the life she'd built for herself in the city. She had no energy right now to fret about it. Perhaps she'd go during the week and pick up some heartworm pills at the vet for Cordite—there was only one left.

The little dog capered in front of her on the trip to the back door. As soon as she opened it, Marmalade, an oversized orange tabby cat, and one of the four semi-feral cats that claimed Rose's back porch as their own, hissed and swatted at Cordite. He yelped. PC scooped him up and deposited him safely outside on the stoop.

The door held a cat flap opening to the outside, and the cats came and went at their pleasure. On the rare winter nights when there was an abnormally hard freeze, Rose brought them into the house to stay warm. Because they were only mostly tame, she threw a towel over them before picking them up. Last winter, she accidentally brought in a large opossum, thinking it was one of the felines. The marsupial was startled, but grateful for the warm bed and cat food dinner. Rose named her Blossom, and she still lived underneath the porch, enjoying a nightly meal of table scraps and cat food, much to Cordite's consternation. Her children and grandchildren showed up when it was very cold to sleep in the empty cat beds.

A glance showed PC the cat feeder was empty. "I'll be out in a minute, Cordie."

She had to move a rocking chair to get to the tall utility cabinet that held the metal bin containing the open bag of cat food. When she did, she bumped into the cabinet, and a cardboard tube fell on her head.

"Ow!" It hadn't actually hurt, just startled her.

The picture on the bottom end of the tube was a 2" x 3" thumbnail of an oil painting, along with the words *Mirabella County Historical Society, QPHS, Battle of Mirabella Creek - Lamartine*. PC scanned the top of the cabinet and saw two more poster tubes precariously perched along the edge. She pulled them down and found they had similar labels but different pictures. One was *Courthouse—Lamartine*, and the other was *Possumwood Tree in Spring—Delgado*.

Best get the critters fed. I'll ask Mama about this when I get done. And the sooner I put the chain on the gate, the better.

Mmmmaaa! Mmaamma! Hazel wasn't too bad, but if the donkeys got started...

Heeyaw! Heeyaw! Heeheeheeyaw!

PC felt sorry for the neighbors. She gave a quick glance over to the Youn's house, half expecting to see Hiro Tran's police cruiser, as his fiancée, Annie, lived there. The street was empty.

"Hush! I'm not going to get there any faster with you yelling at me," she admonished the livestock.

Once the feed was in their bins, they left her to her thoughts. Scooping poop was both mindless and rhythmic, and she found it to be a smelly meditation. The manure pile near the back gate was getting large. Rose's friend, Justice Johnson, collected it for her mushroom farm, but she apparently hadn't come in a few days. Perhaps PC should check on her and make sure she was all right. She was younger than Rose, but not by much.

Speaking of people she needed to check with... Truman Parker had been happy enough to throw Tim Kowalski under the bus, while neglecting to mention that he, too, had had a fight with Roger Haney. What was that about? Parker skinning Roger alive was probably not a serious threat, but what had angered him? Maybe she could find out tomorrow afternoon.

Tim Kowalski had no motive to kill Roger. In fact, Roger stood more to benefit by getting rid of Tim. Tim had, after all, caught him both shoplifting and trespassing. What did Roger think he'd find at Phineas Scott's house? Why did he want a pipe locator?

Jim Hargraves was Roger's best friend. They'd had a tiff about Roger trying to get Jim to help him break into Ada Dotson's house, but if there was any other bone of contention, neither Jim nor Winnie had mentioned it. Both had noticed Roger acting strange lately, though.

Stanley Zimmerman. What did Roger need with ten-thousand dollars? Was he being scammed, as his cousin had thought? Or did this have to do with his secret plan? Why did he think he'd have the money to pay Stan back in two weeks? That part *did* sound like a scam.

Terry Gillespie. He was just trying to protect his girl and Roger was acting kind of hinky. PC cringed. Rose did not belong in anyone's love triangle. People have been getting their competition out of the way for as long as there's been romance—but she didn't think Terry was jealous of Roger. No, more that he wanted to shield Rose from Roger's unwanted attention. The need to protect could be a powerful motive, but PC wasn't convinced it would drive Terry to do Roger in. However, he did have both means and opportunity. But the one thing that screams it wasn't him is the musket ball. Hard to believe Terry would shoot him with a 100% identifiable round. That smacks of a setup. But then again, people do stupid things when they're in the throes of emotion.

Who else would want to kill you, Roger?

Someone from the Historical Society? Someone at the library or courthouse who felt nagged to death by his incessant research? Did he owe the wrong kind of person ten large? Scammers often made threats, but they typically lived nowhere near their victims, so the threats were not worth the electrons they were emailed on. Loan sharks tended to beat people up, not stealthily plan a murder and frame someone else. Did he need surgery? He was more than old enough for Medicare. Roger was desperate enough for a pipe locator that he was willing to shoplift one. Is there something that costs ten grand that he's willing to beg, borrow, or steal to get? That seems the most reasonable. But what is it?

I sure hope some fresh evidence comes to light, because Terry's looking like the most viable suspect. Him being the killer would just break Mama's heart, and that's the last thing she needs while she's healing up from her surgery.

PC's brain was still trying to shake some clues loose from the available information as she made her way into the house. She picked up the three poster tubes and carried them inside.

"Mama? Where did you get these?"

Rose craned her neck around the recliner. "What's that?"

PC held the tubes out to her mother.

Rose studied them for a long moment. "I'd forgotten all about those! I'd meant to get them framed way back when. The Historical Society sells prints of a lot of pictures they have on exhibition. I got those at the Quenton Plantation, but I think they might have a thing where you can order 'em over the internet."

"Thanks."

PC had just dropped the tubes on her bed and was about to undress for the shower when her text chime sounded.

It was from Tran. "Phineas Scott's house. ASAP."

Chapter 9

PC CIRCLED THE block, looking for a place to park at Mayor Phineas Scott's house. Woody's official Tahoe, along with three police cruisers, was in front of the house. The only parking spot was along North Cumberland, which was parallel to Scott's home. Officers milled around in the back yard.

Tran met her at the gate. "That was quick."

The detective looked over his shoulder into the yard. "What's going on?"

Tran led her past the huge live oak to the old well. The concrete planter had been shoved onto the ground, the bright pink and white petunias spilled and trampled into the grass. The chain that held the wooden cover on had been severed, and a bolt cutter leaned against the well.

"We got a call from a neighbor about a break-in at the mayor's house. A back window had been broken, but we didn't find anyone inside."

"Is Phineas okay? And the dog?"

Tran chuckled. "They were actually out of town for a dog agility competition. He was already on his way back. Should be here in another half hour, give or take."

PC imagined the hairless Anubis running around an obstacle course and wondered if being bald made him faster—like swimmers who shave all their body hair to reduce water resistance.

Tran cleared his throat. "The mayor'll have to confirm whether anything's been taken from the inside—if they wanted something, they knew exactly where it was, because there was no ransacking. But the well... see for yourself."

PC looked down. A camping lantern hung suspended by a piece of cotton rope from the well's spindle, lighting up the deep hole with bright white LEDs.

The figure of a man lay at the bottom of the well. Pieces of a broken, rotting rope ladder were scattered around and on top of him.

"Who is that?"

Tran shrugged. "No idea. Dr. Mack came out with Tibby Brown— the plumber—and they used his pipe snake camera to get a closer look. He said that, based on the clothes and skeletonization of the corpse, he would be surprised if that guy ended up in the well any later than the Civil War. He called in the state archaeologist, and he's bringing a forensic anthropologist from the DPS with him."

"When are they supposed to get here?"

"Well, they're coming from Austin." Tran glanced at his watch. "We called them an hour and a half, two hours ago. Should be any time now."

"I've never seen anything like this before. Does the mayor know there's a skeleton in his well?"

"Not yet."

PC walked around the well, careful not to touch anything. "Wonder why he was down there? It looks like he had a ladder, but it broke and he had no way out. Somebody closed the lid—did he do that, or did someone see him in there and close the lid on him? What would anybody be doing crawling around in a dry well?"

"What if he had a hiding spot? Not everybody has a mattress to stuff his cash under."

PC nodded. "There is a famous missing person case, one hundred and sixty years old."

"Francois de Lamartine?"

"Yeah. He vanished right before the Civil War."

Tran leaned over, peering into the well. "Whenever I heard about that legend, I figured he took any valuables he might have had and fled the country before the war got started. Canada? Mexico? A steamer back to Europe? No telling. But I would never have put 'died in a well on his own property' on my bingo card. That just seems too... anti-climactical."

PC shrugged. "Hasn't been confirmed that's him. Wonder if they'll find any useable DNA? He's got descendants in this area?"

"Probably half the town."

"Donovan? What are you doing here?" Woody's voice made PC jump.

"Evening, Chief. You know I've been looking at those cold case files for you—and this is probably the coldest one you've got. Sooner or later, the truth will out. Looks like something's finally been discovered here."

Woody held her eyes for two moments too long. Then he looked at his hands, stretching the fingers out, then folding them into loose fists. "You're right. Truth always comes out. Sooner or later."

His text chime went off, and he took out his phone. "The ologists are here." He turned and strode to the side gate.

PC watched him go. She thought she still knew him reasonably well. But it seemed like every interaction she'd had with him since she'd been back in Possumwood put her on her back foot. They'd dated for two years in high school, and he dumped her right before the homecoming dance. Even though she'd gotten over him forty years ago, he still seemed to remember how to push her buttons.

He had told her he had to work on the night of the dance, but he'd gone to play pool with his cousin. A disappointed PC had sat at home, her mother letting her win at Chinese Checkers.

Until the call came.

Someone had robbed the family-run convenience store and shot her father. Everything had stopped with that ringing of the phone, and Elwood Wilson was the farthest thing from her mind.

The gate banged, startling her out of her reverie. Woody returned, followed by a man and a woman carrying climbing gear. As they got closer, she estimated the wiry man to be late fifties, early sixties. The petite woman, her brown hair pulled into a messy ponytail, perhaps mid-thirties. They bickered about who was going to get to go down first.

Woody introduced Dr. Ted McIlwraith, State Archaeologist, and Dr. Abby DuPree, DPS forensic anthropologist.

Dr. DuPree won out.

She strapped on her gear and a helmet with a headlamp, while her colleague rigged up the anchor. After a safety check, she sat on the edge of the well and swung her legs over. It didn't take long for her to rappel down the twenty feet to the bottom. PC watched her take photographs and small fabric samples from the skeleton's coat and the frayed rope ladder.

Tran and Dr. McIlwraith hauled her up.

"What do you think?" the archaeologist asked as he put on his climbing harness.

Dr. DuPree unsnapped her helmet. "Based on size and clothes, I'd say male. Right femur and pelvis are broken and displaced. Can't tell if it happened in the fall, or was due to scavenger activity. Not sure what would have gotten in there and back out with the lid chained down, though. Anyway, he's been down there a long time. Those bones are likely to be pretty brittle. We may need to cast him."

"That's going to be tough in this small space."

Then he had his turn down the shaft. Tran and Woody hauled him out after his inspection.

"I think you're right, Abby. Most likely male. Clothes are Civil War era. If we cast him, we'll need a crane to haul him out—that plaster'll weigh a ton." McIlwraith looked from the ancient tree to the extensive outdoor entertainment areas and frowned. "I don't see getting one in here without a lot of property damage."

The wind picked up. Thunder grumbled in the distance behind looming black clouds.

McIlwraith cast his eyes to the gloomy sky. "We don't have time to cast and get a crane. Now that the well's uncovered, he really shouldn't get wet. But I do have an idea."

"What's that?"

"Excuse me, Chief Wilson? Could you get us a backboard and a cadaver pouch from one of your EMT crews? We'll replace it."

Woody nodded and got out his phone.

Tran steered PC away from the action. "We got some results back from the autopsy."

"Let me guess. Acute lead poisoning?"

"Not exactly."

Chapter 10

PC COCKED HER head. "Really? Seems awfully soon to get a tox back. What was in the report?"

Tran's eyes flicked to the well and back to the detective. "Dr. Mack's still waiting on the tox screen. When he opened up Roger Haney, he found most of his remaining blood pooled in his abdomen and lungs. But it hadn't clotted—it was still liquid."

"I've never heard of that before."

"Haney took blood thinners—had to go to his doctor once a week to test the level of warfarin in his blood. Dr. Mack ran that same test, and his level was off the chart. Even if he hadn't been shot, he almost certainly would have died from internal bleeding."

The bruise on Roger's arm. "What do you think that means? Two people who wanted Roger Haney dead, or one person who was taking no chances?"

"That is an excellent question. Sanchez and I are going to look around Roger's house tomorrow afternoon. I think two is probably the earliest we can pick up the keys. You wanna come?"

"Sure. I'll meet you there."

Red and blue strobes flickered across the ancient tree. An EMT jogged through the gate with a backboard and a body bag. Dr. DuPree was already rigged up and ready to be lowered back down into the well.

A raindrop kissed PC's cheek. The angry thunderheads were now overhead, and lightning flashed inside them, desperate for an escape. "I'll be right back."

She trotted out to her vehicle and retrieved the oversized golf umbrella that lived in her car. A fat drop of rain smacked her arm, then another, and another. Racing the downpour, she opened the brolly as she ran, making it to the operation as the bottom fell out of the sky and rain bucketed down so hard that it bounced off the ground, creating a thick mist a foot or so off the grass.

Tran ducked under the nylon canopy. "Good thinking."

PC sheltered the well as much as she could with the umbrella. Most of it was covered, but that meant that frigid rainwater splashed down her and Tran's backs. They both strained their necks to see what the anthropologist was doing.

McIlwraith lowered the cadaver pouch and backboard down after her. Carefully, she slid the skeleton into the body bag, moving it as little as possible. Then she unclipped a roll of twine from her belt and tied it around the container, apparently to keep the fragile bones from sliding around in the pouch. Once she was satisfied with the twine, she picked up the wrapped body bag and carefully strapped it to the backboard, which was dangling vertically down the shaft.

Dupree gestured for them to lift the backboard, jerking her thumb up. McIlwraith and one officer pulled it up. Once it was clear, they pulled the anthropologist out of the well. PC held the umbrella, Tran huddling close to her, while DuPree shucked off her climbing gear and got it packed up. McIlwraith and Woody had already taken the body to the archaeologist's van. There was no point in trying to talk—the rain roared down on them like a dozen freight trains. DuPree gave them a smile and a thumbs up, then sprinted through the deluge after her colleague.

PC pointed to the covered outdoor kitchen a few yards from the house and they splashed their way to it. It was drier than standing out in the yard, because rain wasn't falling directly on their heads, but it splattered in at the open sides. The torrent on the metal roof was deafening. They were both already soaked to the skin from the derriere down. Tran gestured to something on the table.

Shattered glass and splintered wood were strewn across the tile. A fist-sized landscaping rock lay next to it. Tran pulled his phone out of his breast pocket and snapped some photos. They both searched the kitchen but found nothing else obviously out of place. He nodded toward the home, and PC agreed. They made a run for the back steps of the elegant Victorian veranda. It wrapped around the house, so they used its shelter to get to the front door. She hung her umbrella by the handle loop from some wrought iron scrollwork, and they hurried inside. It was much quieter in there—two stories between the ceiling and the roof baffled the noise from the downpour.

Anubis growled. His blue-black, hairless skin glistened in the light of the chandelier, and his bat-like ears pricked forward.

Woody glanced over at them, and Mayor Phineas Scott stroked the dog's bald head. "Shhhhhh. It's okay, Nubie."

He quieted, but PC could feel yellow canine eyes boring into her, unwelcoming, and it gave her the willies.

Scott's mouth dropped open, and he raised his hands, palms out, as if warding off a charging toddler. "Stay right there!"

He trotted down the hall, returning moments later with two oversized beach towels. His eyebrows arched as he handed one to each of them. "Stand on these."

It was only then that she noticed the chief standing on his own beach towel island. She had to look down before she laughed out loud.

Scott, who wore a cotton batik print shirt in clashing colors, pursed his lips. "I'm sorry. I don't want you dripping all over my wood floors. I've just had them sanded, but they haven't been sealed yet. They were supposed to have finished that before I got home. As I was saying, Chief, the only thing that seems to be missing is a shadow box display of some antique brass and iron keys."

PC and Tran looked at each other, then Tran pulled out his phone. "Could it have been this?"

The mayor studied the smartphone screen. "Frame is the same type of wood."

Woody shuffled his towel around to face them. "Where did you find this?"

"Outdoor kitchen," Tran replied.

"When this rain lets up, Phineas, will you walk around with us outside and point out anything missing? Or extra?" Woody pulled his own phone out of his pocket.

Scott's fingers trailed over the dog's head. "Of course."

The men continued talking, but PC was only dimly aware of the sounds of their voices. She muddled her towel along the floor to stand in front of the stone fireplace in the formal living room. Above it hung an oil painting of the mansion. The plants were different, but the house was the same—a three-story baby blue Victorian with white trim and a mansard roof. The painting was large, about 4' x 3'. The brass plaque on the frame read, *La Belle Dame Bleue*.

A Francois de Lamartine original.

As she got closer, she spotted what she was looking for. The woman in blue. This time, she stood on the widow's walk that crowned the roof, hanging snowy cotton sheets on a clothesline. A cardinal perched on the white scrolled railing, watching her.

"Phineas? Is it okay if I take a few pictures of this painting?"

He looked at her quizzically. "As long as you don't use the flash."

PC nearly tripped over the coffee table as she backed up to get the full picture. Then she zoomed in on quadrants, and finally, the lady in blue. She stared at the woman in her cerulean dress, a white apron furled by the breeze, doing yet another patently absurd thing.

Who are you? What are you? Some kind of code?

"Donovan!" Woody's raised voice made her jump. "Will you be joining us outside? The rain's down to a sprinkle and I'm fresh out of engraved invitations."

PC shook her head to get her bearings. "Sure, Chief."

The rain may have slacked off, but heavy, dark clouds suffocated both the fading sun and the emerging stars. Twilight had been skipped in favor of going straight to relentless night. Tran and the other uniformed officers used their MagLites, but hers was at home and she had to content herself with her cellphone flashlight.

Having already scoured the kitchen, she entered the gazebo. There was an empty soda can on the floor, and next to it, an unopened single-serve bag of chips. If someone wanted to remain unseen, sitting on the bottom of the gazebo would do it. The solid wood sides blocked the view from the road and the house, with the koi pond bridge between the gazebo and kitchen adding another layer of opacity.

"Tran! Come check this out."

Her friend started jogging over the rain-slicked bridge toward her. His feet slid in opposite directions, and he danced like an electrified spider, trying to keep his balance as his shoes skidded over the slippery wood. His powerful flashlight tumbled into the fishpond.

"Are you alright?" PC hurried over to him.

"I'm good, but this thing is slicker than owl snot."

The waterproof flashlight glowed like a tiny sun on the pond's floor. A drowsy goldfish drifted by. PC's eye caught a glint of metal among the aquatic plants.

"What's that?"

Using both side rails, Tran gingerly finished his ill-fated bridge crossing. He came and stood next to PC. "Looks like an old-timey key."

Tran lay on the edge of the pond and reached in to retrieve his MagLite and the key, but the water was a little too deep.

He sighed. "I was just starting to dry out."

He took off his boots and socks before stepping into the pond. He grabbed the flashlight.

PC pointed at the shimmering metal. "Looks like there are several keys."

He swept up the gleaming objects and hoisted himself out of the pond, four keys in his left hand. They were heavy, the kinds that could be found in the 'Miscellaneous' case at an antique shop. Two were black iron and two were a dark, antique brass. The iron ones had plain loops on the end, but the brass ones had filigrees and swirls, each having a different pattern.

PC inspected them while Tran put his shoes back on. "Wonder if these are from the mayor's missing display case."

Tran texted Woody and asked him to bring Phineas Scott out to the fishpond. The mayor avoided the slick bridge and came around on the grass.

PC gave a half nod and a polite smile. "Phineas? Can you identify these keys?"

His eyes followed her gesture to the freshly retrieved objects. He studied them for a moment. "They could be the ones from my display. I see them every day, but I don't think I could swear to the shapes, I mean there were two black ones on one side, two brass on the other, and a silver one in the middle."

"Are you sure you got them all?" PC looked at Tran.

"Positive."

Scott shook his head. "I don't understand. Why are they out here?"

"We found these four in the pond." PC glanced at the keys. "Do you know what any of them opened?"

"No, not really. Those kinds of locks haven't been on the doors since the 1900s. And I upgraded to smart locks when I bought the house. Besides, that's something the Historical Society put together—it was a house-warming gift from them."

PC gnawed the inside of her cheek. "Was there any kind of label or note in the display case?"

Scott shrugged. "Don't remember."

"Can you describe the silver key?"

The mayor thought for a few moments. "The end was different from the others. But I don't recall much else. I really need to take Nubie out to pee." He turned on his heel and headed back to the house.

PC looked over at the outdoor kitchen. "They're still photographing. Could we have another look at the wreckage before they bag it?"

One officer snapped pictures on his cell phone, while a second officer made notes. When they were done, PC and Tran picked through the rubble before it was bagged as evidence. Underneath the table, she discovered a yellowed piece of paper that had been typed on a manual typewriter—she could see where a correction ribbon had been used, and then the next words didn't quite line up. It read, 'Original keys FRANCOIS DE LAMARTINE HOUSE. Circa 1840.'

She wondered if Dinah Mae Brown, the president of the Mirabella County Historical Society, would be aware of the key display. But given how old the paper was and how faded the type was, it had probably been put together before she was even a twinkle in her mother's eye. But there was one person who might be able to tell her. And she planned to pay him a visit tomorrow, right after she found out why Truman Parker was threatening to skin Roger Haney alive.

Chapter 11

"DIVINITY!" TRUMAN PARKER opened the metal tin that PC handed him. "Is this your mama's secret recipe divinity fudge?"

"You know it is. She feels bad that Guinevere keeps sneaking out to eat your roses." It was her mother's secret recipe, but PC was the one who stayed up until late in the night making it. She was halfway through the first batch when she dropped the candy thermometer and broke it, and her initial guess at 'hard ball stage' was way wrong.

"Well, that is mighty kind of her." He started to back into the house.

"Mr. Parker, could I talk to you for a minute?"

His face fell. "Bitsy? Could you come here, darlin'?"

Parker's plump wife, who made PC think of Mrs. Claus, appeared in the entryway.

He put the lid back on the tin. "Rose Donovan sent over some of her special divinity. Can you take this in the kitchen and pour us some iced tea? I'll be in directly."

She pushed her thick glasses back up her nose before giving PC a shy smile and a tiny wave. Bitsy took the tin and shuffled down the hall.

"Now, what is it you wanted to talk about?"

"It seems you had an altercation with Roger Haney yesterday. You threatened to skin him alive, apparently."

Parker scowled. "Roger said he thought it might look more dramatic and realistic if we tripped at least one of the horses as the cavalry galloped off. I told him no, it was not gonna happen. It's too dangerous, and it was a flat-out dumb idea. But then I found that rope—he was planning to do it anyway, without even telling anyone. Could have got somebody killed doing that, not to mention broken one of my horses' legs. Just glad I found it in time. Roger's not a bad guy, but he can get some crazy ideas."

"So I've heard. Listen, I need to get going. I got a chain and a snap for the gate, like you suggested, so hopefully that keeps Gwen at home. Anyway, I hope you and Mrs. Parker enjoy the fudge."

He waved and retreated into the house.

PC got in her car, intending to run errands. But when she turned onto Travis Street, Uncle Raymond's car was parked in front of Rose's house. She stopped, hoping to find out what was going on with Terry.

When she came in, Uncle Raymond was sitting on the sofa, talking to Rose.

PC hung her car keys on the little hook by the door. "So, what's Terry's status?"

Cordite looked up and half-heartedly wagged his tail. Raymond was rubbing the dog's ears. "It's nice to see you, too, Primrose. The chief wanted to hold him for the full seventy-two hours, but there wasn't enough evidence to charge him. I pointed out that Terry was on several life-saving medications, and if he suffered any adverse health effects due to this ham-handed investigation, the City of Possumwood would be 100% liable. The DA fetched him from the holding cell himself. That Travis Bailey is something else."

"Where is Terry now? Is he okay?" PC glanced around the room, as if he might be lurking behind the couch.

"It was really late when I got him home last night. I made sure he took his pills and let him go to bed. I expect he's having a lie-in this morning. But I planned to check on him. Thought my sister would want to come along."

PC turned to her mother. "Your chair's in my car. I can push you over to Terry's, then Uncle Raymond can get on with his day once he looks in on his client."

"I'll be fine with my walker."

"The orthopedist said thirty days. You're not even a third of the way there."

Rose huffed and glared, but PC didn't budge. "Fine, Primrose. Have it your own way."

PC stopped and her forehead wrinkled. "Where's Rocky?"

"He's started volunteering at the Methodist Church food pantry. There's a man—named Kyle, if I remember correctly—that's started coming to Rocky's Tuesday night meetings, and he needs a sponsor. I think your brother sees a lot of himself in Kyle, and he's been trying to help him out."

"That's great. I'm glad to hear it."

Rose bit her lip. "I don't know about that. From what Rocky tells me, Kyle's in a bad place right now. I worry he's gonna drag Rocky down there with him. Truth be told, I would not be heartbroken if Kyle drifted on down to the next town sooner rather than later."

"Oh." Rocky was in a shaky enough state as it was. At the moment, he was working, and he'd been sober almost four months. But that could all change with just one friendly beer. That's one reason she couldn't just go back home to Houston and let Rocky look after their mother. He worked all day at the nursing home during the week, and sadly, PC wasn't sure his sobriety would last. It hadn't before. She'd speak to him later, but she urgently needed to talk to Terry. Rose needed some reassurance, though, even if PC didn't entirely feel it.

"Mama, Rocky's been doing good. He's working, hasn't been hanging out with his old friends, and he hasn't been drinking. He's going to be fine."

Rose gave her a half-hearted smile.

PC squeezed her mother's shoulder before turning away. "Uncle Raymond, would you please help Mama? I'll get the doors."

Terry lived two houses down, so they walked, or rode, in Rose's case. As the trio turned up the sidewalk, PC eyed the Spanish ranch-style home and frowned. There was no ramp up the three steps to the flagstone patio that spread out next to the turret-like entry that was at right angles to three arched windows. For good measure, he'd added a rock garden with cacti and a wicked Spanish dagger yucca plant that loomed threateningly over the steps.

Homegrown security system?

Rose took her brother's arm and PC folded up her wheelchair. The three of them had to go single file up the steps to avoid the sharp spines of the yucca.

Raymond rang the doorbell. PC could see movement behind the small beveled-glass window in the top of the door.

Rose shook her head. "He never locks it." She turned the knob and pushed it open.

There stood Terry Gillespie, wearing nothing but boxers and an open bathrobe.

He seized Rose and kissed her. For a long time.

PC cleared her throat. "That hip's still pretty fragile, remember?"

Terry and Rose released their lip-lock and slid apart. He took her free hand and led her inside. "You sit in the power recliner, my beautiful Rose."

Once she was ensconced in the electronic leather chair, he turned to Raymond and PC. "I just started some coffee. Would you like some?"

Raymond shook his head. "I just wanted to check on you and make sure you were still well and healthy this morning. I will leave you in the very capable hands of these young ladies." He bowed slightly and left.

The detective swallowed hard as she watched Raymond retreating down the walkway. His presence had been a buffer between old and new family dynamics. It was weird for PC, seeing her mother with her boyfriend. Part of her was delighted that her mother had met someone who made her happy. Part of her felt betrayed, almost like Rose was cheating on Trey. He wouldn't want her to be unhappy, and she'd been alone for a very long time after he died. But it still felt awkward and not-quite-right. PC didn't dare leave, because those two clearly needed a chaperone. Her mother might be willing to risk her hip, but the detective wasn't about to let that happen. She pushed her discomfort aside and turned to Terry with a smile.

"Yes, please, on the coffee. Cream, no sugar."

"Coming right up." He disappeared into the kitchen.

"You comfortable, Mama?"

"Yes, Primrose."

"Okay, Mama. Don't even think about it. I'm not leaving you here unsupervised. Besides, how would you get home?"

A sly smile eased over Rose's lips. "Well, I could spend the night."

"Could we please just get your hip healed before you start acting like a boy-crazy teenager? Besides, you have your own medications to take."

Rose pouted. "Daisy would let me stay."

"And that is exactly why *I* am taking care of you and not my sister."

Terry breezed into the room with a tray of steaming mugs of coffee. Much to PC's relief, he'd also gotten dressed. "I'm not interrupting anything, am I?"

"Of course not!" PC blurted, then stopped herself from saying anything more incriminating.

Terry set the tray on the coffee table and gave a mug to Rose. Then he picked up the other two and handed one to PC.

She took a sip and breathed in the vanilla-tinged aroma of the coffee. "How are you doing, after being in lockup all afternoon?"

"I sure am glad Rose sent her brother to help me out. I'd like to think that everybody knows me. Knows I wouldn't hurt a flea, much less Roger Haney. The chief himself came to question me."

Rose giggled. "Primrose here used to date him."

"Mother! That was like forty years ago. Terry doesn't want to hear about ancient history."

"Well, a love life would do you good. Romance keeps you healthy, you know." Rose and Terry shared a meaningful look.

PC looked down and rubbed her eyes. "Mama, this is not the time or place."

"Well, I still haven't 100% forgiven him for not coming to the funeral. But I think Drew Burlesconi is a much better match, anyway."

"I agree," Terry piped up. "Have you seen the way he looks at her?"

"Mama, if I leave, you're coming with me. And I'm not going to sit here and have my love life analyzed by you two. Could we please just talk about something sensible?"

"What did you have in mind?" Rose had a sip of coffee.

"Not this." PC shook her head. "I know. How about the murder that happened yesterday? The one that Terry was detained for questioning about? The one that's going to get pinned on him if we don't figure out who really did it?"

"I'm glad somebody in the police department is on my side."

PC ran a hand through her hair. "While I have done some contract work for Possumwood PD, I wouldn't say I'm in the department, per se."

He looked at her earnestly. "Why do you think I'm innocent when your pals are so sure I'm not?"

PC considered her words. "They don't investigate very many murders here. You had a motive—although I don't think it's a strong one. Roger was harassing your girlfriend, and you wanted to protect her; means—you knew how to load and fire the gun and had it with you at the re-enactment; and opportunity—no one would be able to hear and identify a live round in the barrage of gunfire. But it doesn't make any sense that it was you. Actors aren't allowed to bring live ammo to the event. Even if you found that you mistakenly had one in your pocket, you'd know to set it aside. The shooting wasn't an accident. Everything about this crime looks planned and premeditated. And if you were doing the planning, why on earth would you use a round that could easily be identified as yours? Plain ones were readily available. That would have been profoundly stupid." *Besides Terry, I've met a lot of killers, and you're no killer.*

"I didn't shoot Roger. Even if you believed I engineered it, all you would have to do is talk to Jim Hargraves or Tom Wharton. I can barely hit the target when we go shooting. To ensure I hit Roger, I'd have to fire from point blank range. I was on the opposite side of the group, at least a hundred feet away. I would have had to turn around and fire into all the players. With that black powder smoke, I probably wouldn't even have been able to see him. It would take Lee Harvey Oswald's magic bullet to dodge around the other re-enactors and only hit Roger."

There's that, too. There was no gunpowder tattoo encircling the wound. Roger hadn't been shot at close range. "Is there any way you could draw me a map showing where everyone was standing?"

"I can show you where they started out, but I don't know where they ended up."

"I understand. Anything helps."

He found a piece of paper and searched for a pencil. PC's phone rang. *What does Daisy want?*

"I'll take this outside." She answered as she made her way to the front door.

"What's up, Daisy?"

"The boys and I stopped by to see Mama on our way home from church, thinkin' we might all go for lunch. Where is everybody?"

"Rocky's volunteering, and Mama and I are at Terry's."

"Is he fixin' y'all lunch?"

PC rolled her eyes. "Where do you want to eat? I can ask them if they're up for it."

"Tyson said he had a cravin' for the Brisk Rib." She sighed. "That boy'd prob'ly eat a whole brisket by himself, if they let him. Good thing for the Smiths it's not a buffet."

"I'll ask and call you right back."

An antique black sideboard with a tall mirror crouched against the curved wall opposite the front door in the round entryway in Terry's house. Among the handful of knickknacks, a pewter elephant stood out. It had a feathered headdress set with pink and purple rhinestones and raised its trunk proudly above a green glass bowl that held a set of keys. Given Terry's penchant for loud, flashy clothes, it wouldn't surprise her in the least to find out he'd worked in a circus at one time.

Terry looked up from his map sketching when PC returned to the living room. She chewed her thumbnail.

"Do you always leave your keys in that bowl near the front door?"

His pencil stopped scratching. "All the time. That's why I got so flustered when I couldn't find them yesterday morning."

"Where did they turn up?"

"On top of the gun safe. I must have not put them back after I finished packing my cartridges Friday night and put them away."

"I see. Anyway, that was Daisy. She's asking if we're interested in meeting her, Tyson, and Zach at the Brisk Rib for lunch."

Terry tapped his pencil on the table. "Sure. I'm almost done—give me another five minutes or so."

Rose hugged herself. "Oh! I haven't been to the Rib in ages. Sounds like a nice family lunch."

PC rang her sister. "We'll meet you there. Leaving in about five minutes, give or take."

"Is Terry coming?"

PC wasn't sure if Daisy sounded hopeful or apprehensive. "Yes."

"Alright. See you there. We'll get a table."

PC put her phone in her pocket. "Let me clear away the coffee cups while you're finishing up." She put the empty mugs on the tray and carried them back into the kitchen. After setting the dishes in the sink, she noticed two prescription pill bottles on the breakfast table. Moving to the side so she wouldn't be noticed from the living room, she picked them up. One was atorvastatin.

The other was warfarin.

Chapter 12

TERRY SAID HE didn't *shoot* Roger Haney. And PC believed him. But had he slipped Roger an extra pill or five, and then ironically, been framed by the shooter? Worse yet, were they working together? Terry didn't seem like a killer, but he could be an accessory. Or maybe he was completely innocent. Given the older population of Possumwood, probably at least half the people in this town took blood thinners.

One more question added to the list, and PC was already frustratingly short on answers. She set the pill bottles down quietly and took a breath to compose herself before walking back into the living room.

PC smiled. "I'm ready whenever you are."

"I'm just about done."

"How about I help Mama to the car while you're finishing up the sketch?"

"Sure. That'll work."

Rose pushed a button on the chair's remote, and the seat lifted to gently push her out of the recliner.

She grinned. "We should probably get one for home."

"That looks handy." PC nodded.

Rose was belted in and cold AC was blowing when Terry climbed into the back seat next to her. He leaned forward and handed PC his drawing of the re-enactment.

Can I trust this? PC wondered as she smiled and thanked him, then shifted the car into reverse.

She wasn't in the mood for a family lunch. Any time Daisy came by for a visit, there was going to be some drama involved, and PC had enough on her plate right now. She just wanted to be alone, to think and try to puzzle out the clues. There were still too many missing pieces for a solution, but she could generate some scenarios to test. Guilt gnawed at her for not being excited to see her sister and nephews, but she also didn't have a lot of time to find Roger's killer, and either save Terry from being arrested for a murder he didn't commit, or save her mother from dating a killer. That just seemed more urgent than whatever Daisy's tabloid tale was likely to be. PC clenched her jaw.

The fake smile that PC had plastered on her face when she had taken Rose to the car at Terry's house remained intact as she pulled into the second to last available parking space at the Brisk Rib. It fell when she saw Daisy's geriatric red Impala. A deep scrape ran down the rear passenger door and the quarter panel was missing. The back bumper tilted at a crazy angle.

Rose was turned toward the center of PC's SUV, jawing with Terry through the gap in the front seats, and PC hoped to keep her from looking out the window. She'd be upset if she saw the state of Daisy's car.

"I'm going to get your chair, Mama. Looks like a long line inside. You just sit in the AC for a minute while I get it set up."

Terry unbuckled his seatbelt. "Let me help you."

"No! No, it's fine. Just takes a sec."

He stayed seated and kept talking to Rose while the liftgate opened. When PC brought the wheelchair around, she had to stand at an awkward angle to keep herself between Rose's line of sight and Daisy's crinkled car.

"What is wrong with you, honey? Could you move out of the way?" Rose grumbled as she clambered out of the passenger seat.

"I'm just trying to stop the chair from rolling while you're getting in, that's all."

"It has brakes."

"You can't be too careful."

Rose grunted as she twisted and sat down. PC pulled the chair backward instead of turning it around. She noticed Rose's head shaking, but explaining things would only make it worse.

"Hey, is that Daisy's car?" Terry pointed.

PC shot him a sub-zero glare. He must have snapped to what PC was trying to do, because he said, "Oh, never mind. That's not it."

Rose frowned. "Oh, honey. You know she's supposed to meet us here—"

She stopped herself when she caught sight of the violated vehicle. "Oh, my. I hope everybody's all right. They woulda called if anybody went to the hospital, right?"

"Mama, Daisy said it was her and the boys meeting us. They're all fine. Or at least well enough to chew on some barbecue."

"I'm sure you're right," Rose said, although her hands were twisting and wringing in her lap.

PC was dismayed to see a line of people through the glass door. The detective wasn't sure there was room inside the restaurant for them to stand in line, and she almost suggested trying a different place to eat. Luckily, there was only one couple in line behind Daisy, Tyson, and Zach.

Daisy leaned around the woman, who was dressed for church. "Oh, Mama! It's so good to see you!"

PC smiled through clenched teeth. "Daisy, why don't you let these people go ahead of you, and we can all order together?"

"Of course!" Daisy gestured to the person ahead of her. "Y'all please go ahead."

The man loosened his tie. "Thank you."

Zach moved back to stand next to PC. "Hey, Aunt P."

Tyson was busy playing with his phone, and Daisy pinched his arm to get his attention. He shuffled into place beside his brother.

PC smiled at her nephews. "So, how's school?"

Zach bobbed his head. "S'alright."

Daisy pinched Tyson again, repeatedly, and he put his device away.

PC tried to throw him a line. "School going okay, Ty?"

He made a noncommittal grunt.

Rose petted her younger daughter's arm. "Daisy, honey, what happened to your car?"

"Oh. You saw it?"

Rose leaned forward in her chair. "Yes, and I was real worried for you."

Daisy crossed her hands over her heart and fluttered her eyelids. "It was the strangest thing, Mama. Zachary called me from his job at the feed store. He finished his shift, but the battery in his truck was dead. The jumper cables got left in my car, so I was comin' to see if we could get the dang thing started. I was goin' down North Cumberland, when this truck pulls out of one of them little alley things like the Hounds of Hell are chasin' him and sideswipes me. He didn't even slow down. I had to get out and put the piece that got knocked off in the trunk all by myself."

North Cumberland? That's right by Mayor Scott's house. PC's ears pricked up. "Could you describe the driver?"

"I was too busy trying not to die to pay attention to him. I almost ran into the ditch, and you know how deep that thing is. Nobody'd even see my little car in there."

"How about the truck? Can you describe it?"

"It was black. That's really all I remember."

Not much to go on. Too bad Daisy hadn't gotten a plate number. "Well, I'm glad you weren't hurt. Sorry about your car, though." PC turned to Zach. "Did you get a new battery?"

He nodded. "Yep."

Daisy pinched him, and he rubbed his arm. "Yes, ma'am."

The young man running the register smiled. "Next please! May I take your order?"

PC walked up to the ticket window at the Quenton Plantation Historical Park. The anachronistic pioneer girl was reading on her smartphone, and PC had to rap on the glass to get her attention.

"One ticket?" she asked.

"Actually, I'm here to see Tom Wharton. He's expecting me."

"Okay. I'll tell him."

Moments later, the retired history teacher appeared at the side door of the tiny administrative building next door to the actual antebellum plantation house. PC followed him into his office. It was small, but very tidy. A collection of framed awards and college degrees hung behind his desk.

PC felt like she must be talking to the father of the young history teacher she'd had junior year of high school. But it was a ridiculous thought. Wharton didn't stop aging just because she moved away and didn't see him anymore. Now, he was mostly bald, but the dark grey hair that wrapped from ear to ear behind his head was cropped short, almost to the point of being shaved. His closely trimmed beard and mustache were closer to white than grey, although a few rebellious black hairs fought the good fight along the edges of his sideburns. His bright yellow bow tie with black polka dots was startling against his pale blue Oxford shirt. *All he needs is a tweed jacket and a pipe.*

"Make yourself comfortable, Rosie."

PC sat. "Thanks, Mr. Wharton." She forced a half laugh. "I haven't gone by that name for a very long time. Most people call me PC these days."

"Of course! What can I help you with today, PC?"

"I'd like to talk about Roger Haney." The detective unfolded the sketch of the re-enactors that Terry had made for her yesterday.

There was a knock at the doorframe. Dr. DuPree stood in the doorway. Behind her, Woody towered above the petite scientist.

The forensic anthropologist stepped forward. "We're here for your DNA."

Chapter 13

Tom Wharton stood up. "Ah. I was expecting you a little later. Come right in. What do I need to do?"

DuPree handed Wharton a travel-sized bottle of mouthwash. "We're going to collect your sample with a buccal swab. First, you will rinse your mouth out with water. Once you've done that, swish a capful of mouthwash—you can keep the bottle when you're done—swish the mouthwash around in your mouth for at least thirty seconds. Spit it out, then rinse again with water. It's like a mouthwash sandwich—water, mouthwash, water. Got it? We just want to make sure we get rid of any food particles that might be hanging around out of the way. We don't want to test your breakfast."

"Back in a minute." Tom had to squeeze around Woody, who blocked part of the doorway as he tried not to stand on top of Dr. DuPree.

PC could feel his eyes on her, and she could almost hear the cogs turning inside his brain trying to work out what she was doing here, and if it was relevant to the Haney case. She wondered why he, personally, was driving the anthropologist around.

She put on a cheeky smile and said, "Good morning, Chief. Dr. DuPree."

The scientist studied PC for a moment. "You're the one with the umbrella."

"That's me."

"Thank you so much for that. If those bones had gotten wet, it could have been a real disaster. No telling what kind of mold and fungi spores are on them. I don't believe we were introduced last night."

PC stood up and extended her hand. "I'm PC Donovan."

DuPree twisted her head like a dog hearing a cheese wrapper open. "Police Constable?"

"Detective Sergeant, actually. But PC is short for Primrose Corvina. Always thought Detective Primrose should be a character in a kids' book."

The anthropologist chuckled. "Of course. I probably watch too much British TV."

PC let a small laugh tumble from her lips. "You can't beat *Cracker*, huh?"

DuPree nodded. "One of the classics."

Leaning casually on the back of the chair, PC asked, "Do you have any idea whose bones were in the mayor's well?"

"Not really. We were told that the original owner of the house disappeared in 1860, so we thought we'd start there and collect DNA from his descendants for comparison."

Woody coughed.

If he was trying to prompt the anthropologist into silence, she failed to notice.

"Apparently, M. Lamartine's great-great-great-great granddaughter—Mr. Wharton's mother—is a big fan of Ancestry.com. She'd uploaded all kinds of documents—birth, death, and marriage certificates, property deeds, and even some letters. The Historical Society found a number of Lamartine's kin right off the bat, although I suspect that Dinah Mae Brown probably already knew who they were."

Tom Wharton came back into his office. "Alright. Fresh and clean as a whistle."

"Excellent!" Dr. DuPree snapped on some blue nitrile gloves. "Okay," she started explaining as she took a swab out of a tube and handed it to Wharton. "You're going to take this swab, and holding it flat against the inside of your cheek, I want you to scrub it up and down. Remember, we're trying to collect a good amount of cells, so scrub hard. After you've done that for about thirty seconds, use the clean side on your other cheek." She mimed brushing the interior of her cheek with an imaginary swab, then switching over and doing the other side.

Wharton stuck the swab into his mouth and started to scrub. "Ow!" He pulled it out to look at it.

"Yes, I'm sorry about that. It is kinda like a little dish scrubbie."

Wharton put the swab back in his mouth, rubbing more gently this time. Once he was done, he handed it to DuPree. She returned it to the tube and sealed the swab in.

She tucked the tube into a pouch and gave a cheerful smile to Wharton. "We'll get our samples sent off to the lab first thing in the morning. We might have results in three to four weeks, but six to eight is more common. Unless the lab gets really slammed, then who knows? We appreciate your cooperation. Have a great rest of your day!"

DuPree nodded at PC as she and Woody left the office.

"Bye, Chief," PC called after them.

"Goodbye, Donovan."

She turned back to Tom Warton, to find him probing the insides of his cheeks with his tongue.

"I hope they got enough cells. I think I scraped off the top layer of skin in my cheeks."

PC wrinkled her nose. "Ouch."

"I'm sure it'll be fine. Mouths heal pretty fast. Now. What can I help you with this morning?"

She unfolded the page Terry had given her and smoothed the sketch on his desk. There were about twenty circles, labeled with names, sprinkled through the reconstructed settlement. Five more were on the other side of the creek, as the cavalry—Bill Montoya, Truman Parker, Tom Wharton, and two she didn't know. Terry's circle was one of the closest to the audience. Jim Hargraves, Stan Zimmerman, and Tim Kowalski were all either next to or not far behind Roger, who was about halfway between the middle of the settlement and the water. There were several actors in between Terry and Roger.

There were a number of buildings on the left side, but only one on the right—the dry goods store. Terry had marked that as the control center, where all the re-enactors' gear bags and street clothes were stored during the performance.

"This is a map I got of where the re-enactors started out at the beginning of the event. Could you verify the accuracy for me?"

Wharton looked at it, tracing lines here and there with his index finger. After a minute, he looked up. "Yeah, looks mostly right. I think they were spread out a little more, and Roger and Jim were closer to the store."

"Thanks. My mother goes to the re-enactment every year, so we were there. I can't believe what happened to Roger Haney. We were stunned."

"Yes. It's very tragic. That's why we ban live ammo. Terry Gillespie clearly didn't follow the rules."

"Why are you so sure it's him?"

"It was his musket ball, wasn't it? I've never seen a yellow-orange round anywhere, ever, like Terry's."

"Yes. That's why it makes it so weird that he would use one."

Wharton rubbed his nose. "Never can tell what somebody will do to protect a loved one."

Did Wharton know about Roger's fixation with Rose? "True enough." PC leaned back in her chair. "But Roger clearly had been looking for something. And he apparently thought he might have found it. Do you have any idea what that was?"

"Not sure. But he was obsessed with the lost treasure of Lamartine." Wharton shook his head. "People seem to think Francois came across the pond with some near infinite dragon's hoard of treasure. But as far as anyone in my family knows, he spent any money he brought from France on the house. His cartage business, hauling freight from the steamship port on the Brazos River into Possumwood, then later an import-export venture with some associates in France, was what kept food on the table and that expensive mansard roof over his family's heads. Did you know they imported the blue slate roof tiles from Wales?"

PC shook her head. "So, what happened? How did they lose the house?"

"My great-to-the-fifth grandmother, Hannah Justice de Lamartine—she was somewhat younger than her husband—was left to get through the Civil War on her own after Francois vanished. They did not own slaves. France had abolished slavery, at least on the continent, before Francois was born. But most of the men who worked for the cartage business either fled or left to fight in the war. Blockades stopped overseas shipping cold. While Texas didn't suffer from the scorched earth policies of the Union generals, she was not spared from the economic disaster that was the Civil War and Reconstruction. Hannah had to sell the house and go live with her daughter, Mamie, and her husband, Samuel Wharton. If there had been any treasure, or even money saved from the businesses..." He gestured, palms up.

"Yeah. That would have been prime time to use any gold and jewels that were just lying around the house. It's a great urban legend, anyway—lost treasure from the 1800s."

Wharton smiled. "Sadly, that's all it is."

PC glanced at her watch. It was a quarter to two. She'd have to get this wrapped up soon. "Don't get me wrong, I believe you. But Roger sure seemed to think he was on the trail of something big."

"He might have thought he'd found where the mythic treasure was hidden, but he was destined for disappointment. Poor Roger went through all that trouble to steal those keys for nothing. However, if he discovered my missing ancestor, I'm grateful for that."

"The keys? You mean the ones from the mayor's house? What makes you think it was Roger who stole them?"

"Did you forget you're in a small town? Tim Kowalski had seen him lurking in Phineas' back yard. Who else would it have been?"

"I see your point." PC leaned forward. "But I have another question. What do you know about the Lamartine paintings? He seemed very fond of the Blue Lady."

"Yes. Some people think she's the married mistress, whose husband chased him out of England. She could just as easily be Hannah, his own wife. She's small and in the background. No real details to her face."

"She doesn't seem to fit with the rest of the pictures. She's almost like a… cipher, a code."

Wharton shrugged. "I think Francois just liked surrealism, like Dali with his melting clocks. Perhaps he wanted his own tamer version of it."

Unlikely, since the surrealists didn't show up until the 1920s. "Perhaps. Shame we can't ask him about her, huh?" PC stood up. "Thank you for your time, Mr. Wharton."

She stopped at the ladies' room on her way out. As she washed her hands, she noticed a stem of hay from the morning's livestock feeding tucked behind her ear like a flower.

Classy.

She tossed the hay in the trash and wiped a smudge of who knows what off her cheek.

On to the Haney house. Maybe we'll finally get some answers.

Chapter 14

Tran's cruiser was not in front of Roger Haney's small brick house when PC pulled up in front. It was straight up 2:00, and he was most likely on his way with the keys. She got out to look around.

Roger had transformed his front lawn into a quirky garden collage. He'd built raised beds of various sizes and shapes—round, oval, square, and rectangular. One was an amoebic rock garden with creeping juniper; a massive aloe vera, surrounded by pups; lavender; and a couple of small bushes that looked like they were about to flower at any moment.

A large rectangular bed was bursting with leafy greens—Swiss chard, spinach, purple kale, and a few things PC couldn't identify. A tall circular bed nearby overflowed with herbs—basil, chives, and parsley surrounded a tall, ferny clump of dill in the middle. Oregano, thyme, and mint trailed out of the bed, their leafy stems curling down the brick. In a narrow oval, a yesterday-today-and-tomorrow bush, covered in purple, lilac, and white flowers, was partnered with an angel's trumpet, whose unopened buds drooped like wrong-way okra pods throughout the bush.

In the center of the yard, a wide arbor, heavy with star jasmine, shaded both a birdbath and a bee watering station—a wide, shallow dish filled with clear glass marbles and a small amount of water.

The sound of tires crunching on gravel caught PC's attention. Two PPD squads pulled up behind her SUV. Tran got out of one, and Officer Erin Sanchez got out of the other. PC waved, and Tran returned the gesture before walking to the back of his car to pull his evidence collection kit out of the trunk.

He passed out nitrile gloves and they put them on. Sanchez smiled as she jingled some keys on her way to the front door.

She's so young—looks like a high school student. PC coughed. "Have you done much victimology, Sanchez?"

"Not in the field." She put the key in the lock and opened the deadbolt.

They stepped inside. Tran was only a few paces behind. There wasn't a lot of natural light, so the house was dim. To the left was a formal dining room with a few days' worth of mail stacked on the table.

Jackpot! Maybe.

Past the dining room, the large living room opened on the left, while a door to a hallway yawned on the right. They turned left. The furniture was pretty standard—couch, recliner, bookshelves, television. There was a fireplace, but either he meticulously cleaned it after the last use, or it hadn't been used in some time.

A few pictures graced the mantel and the bookshelves. There were a few of the Zimmerman twins at various ages, and one of Roger and Jim Hargraves holding up strings of fish, but mostly, they were photos of people she didn't know. She guessed the wedding portrait was Roger and his wife, Sonia.

Through the living room was a breakfast nook and kitchen, which connected to the formal dining room. A small bay window above the kitchen sink hosted several plastic bottles overturned on rooting cuttings. On the counter next to the refrigerator sat a half-empty case of ruby red grapefruit.

A trip down the hallway revealed two bathrooms, a bedroom, an office, and a library. There was a sofa in the library, and PC wondered if it was a foldout, in case Roger ever had overnight guests.

The house was mostly tidy. A bit dusty, perhaps, but not dirty, and only a minor amount of clutter.

PC gestured toward the doorway. "We should look at the mail on the table."

Tran and Sanchez followed her into the dining room.

Roger had sorted the mail into three piles: junk, bills, coupons. Next to the stack of bills was a glossy brochure.

"Ground penetrating radar?" PC held it up. "What would he want with that?"

Sanchez and Tran both shrugged.

Tran gestured to the window. "He was going to do a lot of digging in the back yard? He seemed to be flowerbed crazy."

"No. The ones in the front are all raised beds, no digging required." PC looked at the brochure again. "How much do you suppose a ground penetrating radar setup costs?"

Tran took the paper out of her hands. "It says 'call for price.' If you have to ask, you can't afford it."

"I'd be willing to bet at least one of them costs around $10,000."

Sanchez's face scrunched up. "What makes you think that?"

"He was trying to borrow ten grand from the Zimmermans. He also got caught boosting a pipe locator from Justice Hardware."

"How do you know this?" Tran handed the brochure back.

PC smiled. "People like to talk. I like to listen. It probably wouldn't hurt to go through wastepaper baskets, closets, and look to see if there are any file cabinets."

Sanchez twirled the end of her ponytail between her fingers. "What are we looking for?"

"That's a great question. Clues to his personality, activities, associ-ates. It's hard to define, but you'll recognize it when you see it."

PC made her way to Roger's office. Prints of the two Lamartines available from the museum, plus a blown-up photo of the one from the Biersal, hung on the walls. She found nothing unusual in any of his neat folders in the filing cabinet, and no notes explaining his trea-sure hunting theories. After going through his papers, she studied the bookcase. Roger had an eclectic collection of novels and nonfiction, but what caught her eye was a faux leather binder in the middle of the center shelf. At first glance, it could be mistaken for a book, but a closer inspection revealed it was a fake. She pulled it off the shelf and opened it.

Sheet protectors filled the binder, and each sleeve held a photocopy of an old document, probably ones Roger had recently gotten from the courthouse and the library. PC flipped through it and was about to put it back when a loose sheet of paper fell out.

What's this?

The paper had a rough sketch on it of a small room. There was a bench, a wooden chair, and a desk or table. There were no windows or doors drawn in. '$$$! Silver. Latch? Where is 3?' was scrawled across the bottom.

Well, that's clear as mud.

She snapped a picture with her phone before she went in search of Tran, finding him in the master bedroom.

He looked up. "I've found his Coumadin. Nothing else, really."

She handed him the sketch. "What do you make of this?"

"It looks like an office?"

"Possibly, but it's not his office."

"Could there be silver ingots hidden in the cabinet? I mean, there's dollar signs and the word 'silver.' Maybe he hasn't figured out how to open the latch? No idea about the three."

Sanchez strolled into the room. "I didn't find anything. He's got a ton of greens, probably from the garden, in the fridge."

PC ran a hand through her hair. "I believe the radar brochure probably is related to why he wanted $10,000, and why he tried to steal the pipe locator. Not sure about this sketch. It could be nothing, or it could be the location of whatever he was looking for. A cache of silver? What if there's three of them and he thinks he's located two? I've probably seen enough. If I come up with anything, I'll give you a shout."

She left Tran and Sanchez to lock up. Rose needed some things from the grocery store, so PC planned to stop at Marberger's on the way home. As she passed the mayor's house on Main Street, she had a sudden thought. It was Sunday afternoon, so the liquor store wouldn't be open. She might be able to catch Ada Dotson at home and get a look at her paintings—perhaps one was a Lamartine. PC made a quick turn down South Cumberland.

There was no doorbell, so she used the brass knocker.

Clack! Clack! Clack!

Each kiss of brass on brass was like a thunderclap. Not a creature was stirring within. She was about to give up and continue on her grocery run when Ada answered the door.

"There something I can help you with, Detective?"

"Hey, Ada. I know this is going to sound weird, but do you have a Lamartine?"

"A what?"

"A painting. By Francois de Lamartine?"

She stepped aside and PC entered. Ada's huge Maine Coon cat, Hennessy, watched from his perch on top of the elaborate marble in-laid cabinet in the living room. "Why is everyone suddenly interested in this painting?"

"Oh? Who else has been by?"

"Friday evenin', Jim Hargraves, Roger Haney, and Tom Wharton stopped by. They wanted to take pictures, but I wouldn't let 'em. Last night, Stan Zimmerman personally delivered a case of persimmon ale, and spent a while gawping at it. I didn't even order any persimmon ale—nobody buys that stuff unless they're in the Biersal and already half drunk."

PC laughed. "I can believe that. Roger Haney was obsessed with the Lamartine paintings before he died. I was wondering if there were any clues in the pictures that might have set him off on his treasure hunt."

"You can have a look and see what you think."

Ada led her to the formal living room. Opposite the polished gran-ite fireplace, overshadowing a queen Anne settee, hung the Lamartine.

The primary subject was a well. Possibly the one from Phineas Scott's yard. The base was made of fieldstone. A post on either side supported the spindle and a small, pitched roof. Just like the mayor's well. A live oak tree stood off to the side of the structure and a little in front of it.

And there she was. The lady in blue. She was holding a black lace fan. A blue jay perched on one of the lower branches of the tree.

Ada clipped the end off of a cigar. "It's called 'Well Done.' So whadda ya think?"

PC sighed. "It's... a well. The Blue Lady doesn't make any sense to me."

The liquor store owner waved her cigar. "You need to get Tom Wharton and Drew Burlesconi in a room together and ask them about it—Tom knows almost everything there is to know about Possumwood, and Drew knows a lot about art."

"I hadn't thought of that. Might work. Do you mind if I take a picture of your painting?"

Ada considered her cheroot. "Fine. If it will help solve Roger's murder. Although I heard they arrested Terry Gillespie for that."

"They took him in for questioning, but they didn't have any evidence to hold him. I'm not convinced he did it, though."

"I don't suppose you would be."

PC ignored that last remark. She took photos, some of the entire picture, and some zoomed in to quadrants, and of course, a closeup of the Blue Lady section. Then she thanked Ada and left.

By Monday morning, PC still hadn't gotten any fresh ideas as to the identity of Roger Haney's killer or killers. She scooped forkfuls of manure into a wheelbarrow as Rose's menagerie munched their breakfast.

Was it really possible that two people wanted him dead? That seemed extreme, for a retired fellow who liked to cosplay Texas history. There had been no evidence at his house that he was connected to criminal activity. He was just a treasure hunter, and there was nothing illegal about historical research. Maybe he accidentally overdosed himself on his blood thinners, forgetting he'd already taken his pills a few times? How many days would that have to happen?

Regardless of how he came to have a warfarin overdose, someone shot him. Could it have been an accident? If so, somebody would have had to have loaded one of Terry's orange musket balls accidentally, but who had access, other than Terry?

The sound of metallic jangling startled her, then she felt something slide up the side of her butt cheek. She whipped around to see Hazel pogoing off with PC's keys in her mouth.

"Hazel! What are you doing? Come back here with my keys!"

The goat slung them around, apparently enjoying the clash of metal on metal. PC stepped into the feed room to get some cookies. If Hazel got cookies, of course, Guinevere and Arthur were going to demand their share. PC counted out six and dropped them into a feed bucket.

"Hazel! Bring me my keys!" She shook the pail.

The goat stopped and craned her neck. She bounded to where PC was shaking the bucket, keys rattling with every bounce. Gwen and Arthur trotted over to ensure they didn't miss out. She gave the donkeys their cookies. When Hazel opened her mouth to bleat in protest at the unfairness of it all, PC caught the keys before they fell in the mud. She passed the goat the last two treats.

As PC wiped the goat slobber onto her jeans, her silver house key glinted in the morning sun.

"Of course!"

She rinsed her hands under the faucet and wiped them on a slobber-free section of pants. Then she retrieved her phone and texted Tran. "I know who killed Roger Haney, but I need your help to prove it."

Chapter 15

PC AND TRAN walked into the Possumwood PD conference room.

Tran pulled out a chair and sat. "Alright, whodunnit?"

PC roamed around the table. "There are a lot of things that have been bothering me about Terry Gillespie as a suspect."

"Like what?"

"First of all, while he may have had means and opportunity, he didn't really have a motive. Roger was no romantic threat—Mama wasn't remotely interested in him, and Terry knew that. Even if Roger didn't."

"Okay. What else?"

PC took a sip of coffee and set it down on the table. "That musket ball. Terry would have to be dumber than a box of hammers to use one of his own orange specials. Since the crime was premeditated, he could easily have put his hands on a plain lead ball."

"You've got a point, there."

"When we went to visit him after he was released from custody, Mama just walked right on into his house. She said he never locks his doors. Terry arrived late to the re-enactment because he couldn't find his keys. He told us he always leaves them on the sideboard in the foyer, but he found them on the gun safe, making him think he'd been careless. But I think the killer came in the unlocked door while Terry was asleep, opened the safe, took a dyed musket ball cartridge, then relocked the safe and left the keys on top."

"Go on."

"Roger was shot in the chest, not the back, correct?"

"Yeah."

"So that means he was shot by one of the soldiers, not by a settler. The killer knew all about the horses being used in the event, and he switched the jumpier young horse, Mingo, out with the calmer, seasoned horse, Cocoa, so he had the best chance of making his shot. That's why Bill Montoya got on the wrong horse and then got dumped in the creek."

"So, you're saying Truman Parker did it?"

"No. It wasn't him."

Tran leaned back in his chair. "Then who was it?"

"This is what was stumping me. I couldn't figure out who would want to kill Roger or why. There was no evidence he lived a high-risk lifestyle. And while he got into a few spats with his fellow re-enactors, there didn't seem to be any credible threats against him. The missing key from the mayor's house was, well, the key."

"The key?"

"Early Friday morning, Tim Kowalski reported that he saw Roger in Phineas Scott's back yard. Later that day, Roger was boasting that he was about to come into a fortune."

"So, he stole the key and found the secret hiding place? Then what? Someone killed him for the money?"

"No. He couldn't have stolen the keys. There was no break-in Friday morning. The mayor hadn't left for his dog show yet. The burglary happened Saturday afternoon. Roger was already dead by then."

"I'm not following you."

Sirens wailed from the fire department across the street.

Tran's cell rang. "This is Tran… location?… on it." He disconnected and stood up. "There's been a wreck, possible fatality. You want to ride out with me and tell me your theory about who killed Haney?"

"Sure." PC almost backtracked. *Was it worth the risk of getting stranded who knows where at a fatality investigation?* But she thought it was better to go and tell Tran who the killer was than wait. Who knew when they'd come after Terry again?

They hurried out to Tran's squad and buckled up. He pulled out of the lot and lit up the light bar.

"So, you were saying about the keys?"

It had been a long time since PC had been in a police cruiser, running hot down a stretch of empty asphalt. "Right. The keys. Roger was sure he'd found something, probably Lamartine's lost treasure. He'd been spending all of his time either in the library or the courthouse, looking up historical documents. Roger had been keeping his cards close to his chest, but either he told someone, or this person followed what he was doing and figured it out. Who knows more about Mirabella County history than anyone else?"

"Dinah Mae Brown?"

"Even more than her. Tom Wharton, local historian, and descendant of Francois de Lamartine."

"Tom Wharton? How do you figure that?"

"He was the director of the re-enactment. He performed all the safety checks, which gave him the leeway to slip a cartridge with a live round into his gun, and he was one of the horsemen, putting him in the right position to fire the fatal shot. He was very familiar with the horses and switched Cocoa and Mingo at the re-enactment. He's the one who suggested to me that Roger had broken into the mayor's house and stolen the keys, but Roger was on a slab in the morgue at the time of the burglary. The neighbor didn't call to report the break-in until late afternoon."

"I'd have to look at the report. They might have reported seeing someone in the yard, or perhaps they saw the back door open and the broken window, which could have happened Friday night."

"No, it couldn't have. Phineas and Anubis didn't leave until early Saturday morning. Also, somebody in a black truck came tearing out of the alley Saturday afternoon and sideswiped my sister and her kid. She didn't get a good look at them, though. I will bet you money that the driver of the black truck is the key thief, who is also Roger Haney's killer. I fully expect you will find that Tom Wharton drives a black truck, and if you examine the truck, you will find red paint on the driver's side bumper."

"But why? Why would he kill him?"

"Maybe because Roger really had found the Lamartine treasure, and Tom wanted it all for himself? Motive for most murders boils down to sex, money, or revenge. It probably wasn't sex, and if there was bad blood between them, nobody seemed to be aware of it. That leaves money. Unless Tom was a sociopath and did it just because. I guess we can ask him when we pick him up."

Tran slowed. The flashing lights of the firetruck and ambulance up ahead marked the location of the wreck. A plume of white smoke rose above the bridge. PC could smell burned plastic, spent fuel, and scorched paint before Tran even stopped the car. He parked across the middle of the two-lane road, blocking it.

"Alright. Let's see what's going on."

A long, s-shaped skid mark slithered down the road, as if the driver had swerved into oncoming traffic, then lurched back into their original lane. As they neared the scene, she saw that a vehicle had crashed through the guardrail and fallen about thirty feet onto the train tracks below. The fire department was hosing the smoking ruin from atop the bridge. It wasn't possible to tell what make, model, or color the vehicle had been—it was a crushed, burned lump of metal and molten vinyl now. And then PC caught another scent.

Charred flesh.

Her heart sank. Dread clutched at her insides, and she wanted to vomit. Suddenly, she was yanked back in time twenty years. She was working the night shift when she got the call.

There was an accident.

Her fiancé, Mike, had been life-flighted to Hermann Hospital.

She should hurry.

PC hadn't made it in time. They wouldn't let her see his body. She was both angry and grateful for that. She did see his mangled car, though. Saw where they'd used the Jaws of Life to cut him out of it. PC never handled car accidents well after that. Or hospitals.

"Donovan, are you okay?" Woody and three other officers had arrived. He stood over her, shading out the sun. "You look a little green around the gills."

"I'm fine." She swallowed the acid that had risen in her throat. "Thank you." She did not meet his eyes.

The firefighters had stopped spraying the ruined vehicle, so Woody led the way to investigate. She dropped to the back of the group of officers and followed them down the road to the base of the overpass. They turned onto the grass and walked down to the train tracks. There was a wide debris field from where the car had landed. The rear bumper, including license plate, lay on the gravel. Tran radioed it to the dispatcher so she could run the plates.

She radioed back a few minutes later. The vehicle had been a black Ford F-150.

Registered to Tom Wharton.

Chapter 16

PC SAT AT the table, tuning out the surrounding noise. *If I'd just figured it out sooner...*

The body in the truck had been so severely damaged in the fire that it couldn't be identified. The remains were sent to the DPS regional laboratory to see if they could extract DNA. One of the officers found Tom Wharton's damaged watch in the debris field, and a neighbor had reported seeing him loading suitcases into his car when she walked her dog at 4:30 AM. A search of the house revealed that he appeared to have packed hurriedly and fled. All the money had been withdrawn from his bank account by ATM on Sunday afternoon and in the wee hours of Monday morning.

The most damning thing they found at Wharton's house, however, was a Ziploc bag with the words 'LIVE: dyed' in sharpie in Terry Gillespie's handwriting. Three paper cartridges were inside it, and they were heavy enough to indicate they held lead balls.

She'd watched Dr. Mack look around Roger Haney's house. She'd even helped him count the Coumadin pills Roger had and compared it to the prescription date. The right number of pills were in the bottle. When he saw all the grapefruit in the kitchen, he knew exactly what happened. As it turns out, grapefruit interacts with the drug and concentrates it in the blood. That's why his levels were off the chart, and why he bruised so easily. The ibuprofen that Jim Hargraves had given him just made the bleeding worse.

If the location of the long-lost treasure of Lamartine was, in fact, what Roger Haney was on the verge of discovering, then the only two people who knew how close he'd come were dead. PC didn't really believe in curses, but it sure seemed plausible in this case.

Drew set a glass of dark beer down in front of her.

"Thanks."

"Since you and I are the only ones who made it to the Biersal tonight, did you still want to play darts?"

"Well, you can understand why the Hargraves didn't come—Jim just lost his best friend." PC gazed across the room to the portrait hanging near the bar. "What do you know about Lamartine's paintings?"

He took a sip of his own beer and shrugged. "They're locally famous. Other than Mirabella County locals and expats, and possibly state historians, nobody else is too interested in collecting them. To the best of my knowledge, there are only six.

PC counted on her fingers. "There's one at Phineas Scott's house, one at Ada Dotson's house, one here, and two at the Quenton Plantation. That's five. Where's the other one?"

"Couldn't tell you. But I'm pretty sure there are six. I arranged for restoration of the ones at the museum, and I was certain their letter said there were six known paintings."

"Roger Haney didn't seem to know, either. He got photos of the picture from the mayor's house and here, as well as getting the prints from the museum. Then there was his plan to break into Ada Dotson's to photograph her painting after she wouldn't let him earlier."

"I can look through my records when I get to the gallery tomorrow to see if there's a description, but I don't remember seeing one."

"That will be helpful, thank you. What is your opinion of Lamartine's paintings? What's the purpose of the lady in blue? Is she just some pre-surrealist flourish, or is she a clue to something, whether or not it's the treasure?"

"Lamartine was a pretty average painter, as far as technique goes. The 1850s, when he was doing this series, was in the heart of the Realism period in art. Of course, that doesn't mean that every artist only painted in that style, but his paintings are pretty consistent with it. Medieval and Renaissance painters put a lot of hidden meanings into their art, but the openly Symbolist movement didn't happen until well after Lamartine was dead. I think the Blue Lady meant something to Lamartine, but I can't speculate as to what that was."

PC tore a piece off her warm pretzel and put it in her mouth.

Drew took a quick sip of beer and cleared his throat. "So, are you planning to go to the Maifest parade?"

It was two weeks away. Always the first weekend in May. Rose would still be recovering from her last hip procedure. Trying to get her to stay home from a town event would be like trying to put pajamas on a cat.

"Of course, we'll be there. What about you?"

"I've got a booth in the park for the festival. Wilma will be running it mostly, but I'll have to take some shifts. We'll feature local artists, so they're going to come by and have short presentations about their work. And I was wondering…"

PC swallowed her pretzel and washed it down with a swig of beer. She looked expectantly at Drew.

"I was wondering if you've ever worked on a parade float before. I've got to get started on it next week, and I thought, well, I thought you might want to help."

"I have zero experience with parade floats."

"I have a lot. I'll teach you."

"Then how can I refuse?"

Drew raised his glass. "To new partnerships."

PC lifted her own beer.

Hopefully, no one turns up dead at the parade.

If you enjoyed this book, please consider leaving a review at your favorite book site. Reviews help other readers find and enjoy new books!

Other books by Holly Dey:

Manor of Death: The Possumwood Mysteries Book 1

Death on the Half Shell: The Possumwood Mysteries Book 2

Azalea Trail of Death: The Possumwood Mysteries Book 3

Death Re-Enacted: The Possumwood Mysteries Book 4

Death Rides a Bobcat: The Possumwood Mysteries Book 5

Key to Death: The Possumwood Mysteries Book 6

Death Curated: The Possumwood Mysteries Book 7

Pool of Death: The Possumwood Mysteries Book 8

All Death No Cattle: The Possumwood Mysteries Book 9

Death is Lager than Life: The Possumwood Mysteries Book 10

Art of Death: The Possumwood Mysteries Book 11

Little Town of Death-Lehem: The Possumwood Mysteries Book 12

Winter: Boxset Collection Books 1-3

Spring: Boxset Collection Books 4-6

Summer: Boxset Collection Books 7-9

Fall: Boxset Collection Books 10-12

All of the Possumwood Mysteries are available in

Large Print Editions